FOOTPRINTS IN WET CEMENT

PETER WORTSMAN

OTHER BOOKS BY PETER WORTSMAN

A Modern Way to Die, Smallstories and Microtales, Fromm
International Publishing Co., 1991

it – t = i, an artist's book, produced in collaboration with
graphic artist, Harold Wortsman, here and now press, 2004

Ghost Dance in Berlin, A Rhapsody in Gray, Travelers' Tales,
2013

*Tales of the German Imagination: From the Brothers Grimm
to Ingeborg Bachmann*, an anthology compiled, edited and
translated by Peter Wortsman, Penguin Classics, 2013

Cold Earth Wanderers, Pelekinesis, 2014

Brennende Worte, the German translation of *Burning Words*, a
stage play by Peter Wortsman, translated from the English
by Peter Torberg, Kulturhaus Osterfeld, Pforzheim,
Germany, 2014

New York, NY, 1978, a photo essay, with photographs
by Jean-Luc Dubin, and text by Peter Wortsman, Les
Editions Dumerchez, 2016

Selected Translations:

Posthumous Papers of a Living Author, by Robert Musil,
   Volume One of Eridanos Library, Eridanos Press, 1988;
   second edition, Penguin 20th Century Classics, 1995;
   third edition, Archipelago Books, NYC, 2006; *Flypaper*
   (a selection from *Posthumous Papers of a Living Author*),
   Penguin Mini-Classics, Penguin Books, 2011

Peter Schlemiel, The Man Who Sold His Shadow, by Adelbert
   von Chamisso, Fromm International Publishing Co., 1993

Telegrams of the Soul, Selected Prose of Peter Altenberg,
   Archipelago Books, 2005

Selected Short Prose of Heinrich von Kleist, Archipelago Books,
   2009

Selected Tales of the Brothers Grimm, Archipelago Books, 2013

The Creator, a fantasy, by Mynona (aka Salomo Friedlaender),
   Wakefield Press, 2014

Konundrum, Selected Prose of Franz Kafka, Archipelago
   Books, 2016

PRAISE FOR PETER WORTSMAN

"The behavior of the people [in 'Snapshots and Souvenirs'] was wonderfully human and moving—the sort of thing even the best writers find it almost impossible to invent. The unexpected in human behavior is difficult to take out of the air, as opposed to the usual, which anyone can invent. So that it is precisely these unforeseen details which establish the authenticity of the text, and which give it its literary value…excellent."

–Paul Bowles, author of *The Sheltering Sky*

"*A Modern Way to Die* is a fantastic book and I thoroughly enjoyed it. I have never read anything quite like this, but my enjoyment was due to more than just novelty, it was a response to marvelous writing, wonderful craft, and the breath of imagination… [Wortsman] succeeded so well in his craft and art that it reads 'artless' and 'spontaneous,' which to me is the highest of compliments."

–Hubert Selby, Jr., author of *Last Exit to Brooklyn*

"Wortsman achieves a level of spontaneity and accessibility…to which most writers can only aspire."

–David Ulin, *The L.A. Weekly*

"Wortsman hangs with the masters."

–A. Scott Cardwell, *The Boston Phoenix*

"His work reminded me some of E.B. White's *New Yorker* stuff—observations turned into little reads but with a modernist twist."

–Ruth Lopez, *The New Mexican*

"Peter Wortsman, in the light of day, seems able to connect the power of the dream narrative to conscious language to create unique works that walk a curious line between fiction and poetry."

–Russell Edson, author of *The Tunnel: Selected Poems of Russell Edson*

"A darkly comic folktale for a dysfunctional future, or a nightmare fable for disobedient children, Peter Wortsman's *Cold Earth Wanderers* sends a disaffected teenager down the elevator shaft of an up-and-down human habitat cut off from its roots, on an unsettling journey to recover what was lost. Against the myth of mindless upward progress Wortsman pits the subversive grotesquerie of open-ended lateral exploration."

–Geoffrey O'Brien, author of *The Phantom Empire* and *Stolen Glimpses, Captive Shadows*

Footprints in Wet Cement by Peter Wortsman

ISBN: 978-1-938349-59-1
eISBN: 978-1-938349-61-4
Library of Congress Control Number: 2016954855

Cover Design: Harold Wortsman
With photographs and drawings by the author

Author photo: © 2016 Ricky Owens

Layout and Book Design by Mark Givens
First Pelekinesis Printing 2017

For information:
Pelekinesis, 112 Harvard Ave #65, Claremont, CA 91711 USA

www.pelekinesis.com

Footprints in Wet Cement

PETER WORTSMAN

To Claudie, who clears the way for dreaming

Contents

I

STORIES ON THE RUN

II

TRUE CONFESSIONS

III

TRUE ENCOUNTERS

IV

WISE CRACKS

V

DELPHIC TELEGRAMS

"If a cluttered desk is a sign of a cluttered mind, of what, then, is an empty desk a sign?"

attributed to Albert Einstein

Small Wonder, a foreword

An atom of matter is all it takes to make a pretty big bang. $E = mc^2$, the concise epic of the 20th Century, is three letters and a single digit long. The same impatient age that spawned the transistor and the computer chip, the acronym and the one-minute commercial, the information bit, the sound bite, the photo op, and the tweet, also contrived its own narrative form—call it short short, sudden or flash fiction, call it a story in a hurry, or a poem exploding its corset. Bastard child of the prose poem and the wise crack, illegitimate heir to the parable and the allegory, this mongrel darling was raised on a diet of the coarse and the cunning, brash big city bus bumper and subway ads, political campaign promises, dream fragments, one-liners, and over-the-counter painkiller packaging copy. Ever anxious for a quick fix of meaning, posing now as a poem, now as a story, it steals its strength from legitimate forms only to sabotage any underpinnings of legitimacy. Style and length vary with each narrative according to its needs. Soon enough, tomorrow maybe, it will be categorized, neutered and defanged for popular consumption and the college curriculum. But for the moment it is still as slippery as footprints in wet cement.

I

Stories on the Run

Prehistoric

Snakes, lizards and a baby crocodile lodge in the cuffs of my pants. Lightning strikes. I pluck thunder from the sky. The price of each storm is marked with a little sticker. The rain reeks of asparagus piss. If only this were a clean haiku.

Children's Day in the Maldives

It had been a bad time for Tim. Ditched by his girl friend, Tina, suffering the first tingle of a toothache, a sudden crippling attack of lumbago in the lower back, and just that morning having stepped in a fresh heap of dog droppings on his way to the Korean grocery store that turned out to be closed when he got there, the foul scent of which infused his cramped studio apartment, and furthermore facing a disconnect notice from Con Ed for non-payment, all in a flash flood of calamity that threatened to sweep the little that was left of his waning confidence along with it, he nevertheless held firm.

Ailing in body and soul, Tim hobbled to the kitchen alcove, intending at this ungodly hour of 4 A.M.—insomnia was another recent affliction—to fix himself a cup of hot tea, when, glancing at the calendar on the wall, he noticed it was Children's Day in the Maldives. It made him perk up to think that somewhere on this miserable godforsaken planet someone was celebrating. Why not join in? Yes, indeed, why not extend the Maldivian Children's Day festivities to his rented refuge in downtown Manhattan!

The calendar, courtesy of UNICEF, the one thing Tina left him the day she walked out while he was still asleep, with a hastily scribbled note on a yellow Post-it: "There's a world outside your self-obsessed cocoon," was all he had to go on. It would, he decided, if he let it, lead him out of the slump he was in. Each boxed-in date, a window in time and space, announced a distant to do. Not a box was blank. Tomorrow was Joan of Arc Day in France, which gave him a rise, thinking of the pale white, freckle-faced girls in short plaid skirts and bobby socks at the Catholic School of the same name, that had made him briefly consider conversion in early adolescence. The day after that was Ascension, or if you preferred, the Cricket Festival in Italy, followed by the Hindu holy day of Teej.

Tim hazarded a chuckle.

The hell with doom and gloom! From now on, he decided, it'll be non-stop celebration. It didn't trouble him in the least not to have the slightest idea how the Hindus in India did up Teej, or not to know just what Italians did to mark Cricket Day, though he vaguely associated it with the ethereal voice of Jiminy Cricket singing "When You Wish Upon a Star." I'll invent my own rituals, he decided.

On his Maldivian Children's Day Celebration, he resolved, it is customary to drink hot cocoa. Moreover, while dosing two spoonfuls of cocoa powder—it had to be two—and while waiting for the water to boil the reveler customarily rubs his stomach counter-clockwise and pats his head.

And so it went.

In the next fortnight Tim frolicked for each happy box on the calendar: the Caribou Festival in the Philippines, the Jewish Shavuot (which is also, incidentally, Teacher's Day in Belize) and World Communications Day.

Wednesday was Buddha's birthday, and so on Wednesday he sat in a modified lotus position, not quite managing to twist his knees into a proper yogic paperclip, all day under a tall tree, and not just any tree, but the towering "hangman's elm" at the northwest corner of Washington Square Park, refusing to be bothered by beggars, backache, proselytizing Evangelicals and Chasidim, the rapidly dwindling balance in his bank account—he was also unemployed—or anything else. For how could one possibly dwell on such mundane matters on Buddha's birthday?

The following day was Youth and Sports Day in Turkey, and though Tim suffered a sagging gut, not having set foot in a gym since junior high school, and had been mediocre at every game he ever set a bat or racket to, he lit a torch—or rather, worked his way, one by one, through the matches in the matchbook from the Minetta Tavern, a landmark Italian eatery, now defunct, to which he had once taken his ex, striking each with great pomp and holding it aloft as he pranced, in boxer shorts and t-shirt, around his studio apartment, his private take on the Olympic torch passing ceremony.

The day after that was an unnamed National Holiday in the Cameroon, which Tim marked by eating bananas imported from Costa Rica. (Remember, he was the self-proclaimed high priest of all this merriment, he and he alone made and broke the rules.)

There were days like Saturday, when he had oodles of holidays to pick from: Luilak in Holland, the Muslim Eid al-Adha, and Armed Forces Day in the States, among others. Given the Dutch heritage of erstwhile New Amsterdam, feeling more inclined to celebrate Luilak—even though Peter Stuyvesant, the first Dutch governor, had been a rabid anti-Semite—he went out and purchased a dozen yellow tulips which he plunked in a jug and admired all day until the petals dropped.

That Sunday being a big deal in Yemen, a country perennially torn by civil war, as well as the Armenian Pentecost, and Mother's Day in the Dominican Republic, Tim wrapped a bed sheet around his flabby torso and plunked a pillow case on his head—his own private homage to Yemen, a place, he felt, that needed his support.

And so it went, through Pfingstmontag and Slavic Script and Bulgarian Culture Day, to Children's Day in Italy, which came on a Wednesday.

But when Tim woke the following morning and glanced at the calendar, ready to do things up right, he was mortified to find the box blank. Not a party, nothing doing round the globe—just a plain, ordinary, empty, miserable Thursday of the kind he'd known in abundance. And suddenly this whole holiday celebrating business went hollow. All the smiling hurt his cheek muscles. The tingle in his tooth intensified into a full-fledged ache. Tremors of pain shot up and down his back. Wincing, he retired to bed with a scowl of quiet despair, his constant and ever faithful mistress who had been there waiting it out, a flickering candle on the window sill of his heart.

And even though the next day was Children's Day in Nigeria, Tim lay in bed, staring in a paralyzing bout of despondence at the ceiling, where he noticed a new crack radiating outward and a green mold growing since last he looked.

Buster

One day a successful comic book artist bored with the usual superheroes invents one whose role it is to destroy. The character is named The Destroyer, but everybody calls him Buster.

Buster busts up. Sometimes he even busts himself up. Luckily, being invented, he can be re-assembled afterwards or started again from scratch.

Totally unexpectedly, mid-series, Buster turns on his creator and pokes his eyes out.

"How can I continue to draw you now that you've rendered me blind?"

Buster sticks out his tongue, gives the finger and worse. The funny thing is his creator can't see him do it, and can only hear about it secondhand, so to speak, from the invented mouths of other characters he sketches by instinct.

Like Lilly, the Reptile Lady, who is secretly in love with Buster and shows it every chance she gets by sinking her fangs into him.

"Ouch!" Buster grins.

But remember, Buster has superpowers.

Buster does a cosmic karate chop that can split the world in two or send seismic waves clear across creation to be read like Morse code messages by the folks back home on his native planet. This is what they read instead of newspapers and comic books. This is what they do for pleasure and pain, work and play, relaxation and duress. Read and interpret seismic waves sent by a runaway from their world implanted in the brain of a blind cartoonist.

Buster's seismic waves are big hits at home.

Bands set them to music.

Skywriters plaster the horizon with such slogans as: LIVE ON THE EDGE OF A DULL BLADE AND YOU BLEED DULL IDEAS.

Couples reproduce or refrain from reproduction according to those seismic waves, though, of course, every would-be breeder dreams of begetting a Buster.

All speeches and prayers begin and end with references to Buster's destructive potential.

One day the cartoonist runs out of ink.

In a rage he breaks his pen and smashes his ink jar.

That is when, although invisible, Buster is most himself.

The cartoonist is distraught but happy, because Buster is happy and Buster is his reason for being.

The cartoonist knows that one day Buster will be his undoing. But until that day he stains the page with his unrest and wins wide acclaim for creativity.

Conversation Camp

They sent him to a conversation camp because he would not speak. Still he kept quiet. The guards, or interlocutors as they were called, tried to worm the words out of him. *Come now*, they coaxed, *why not speak of the weather*. But he said nothing. His bunkmate, a quiet man like himself, who may or may not have been a covert interlocutor planted to make him speak, proved a comfort and a concern. In response to the man's enquiring looks he shut his eyes tight and pressed his fists hard against them. He had no way of knowing if the man sympathized, as he was in any case replaced the next day by another. And every day the pressure mounted. It acted like a frame or a traffic light, something to bump up against to reaffirm what he had been given to believe, that there were invisible limits, barriers he could not even dream of getting beyond. Even so he had his doubt, and this doubt which he kept to himself, though they knew he had it, became a kind of currency for which he traded certain favors. Doubt fulfilled an unspoken need. A question mark to cling to as the last trace of that outmoded cache of envy and longing called self.

1040

In the early days before they rounded us up, we were let to run wild. Never a day would pass when my friends and I, armed with pocket calculators, would not run out into the fields and inventory the blades of grass—a futile exercise, I grant you, but one that sharpens the actuarial instinct in preparation for important problems to come.

"Albert dear," my father would warn me, "hide your calculator when the artists come, for they will surely take it from you and smash it to bits."

"But why," I pleaded, "do they hate us so?"

My father shook his head and passed a weary hand over his glistening bald pate, where the dread digits 1040 were tattooed. "I don't know, son. It could be," he paused to reflect, "that they are averse to numbers. When I was a boy," he said, beaming as he always did, recalling the days before the world was turned on its head, "accountants were respected members of society and an artist was a sponger at best, a poor wretch who might come knocking at your door to beg a slice of Wonder Bread or the remnant of a TV-dinner, the traditional food of the day, and offer in exchange a pathetic little ditty, a shred of doggerel or an indecipherable drawing scrawled on the back of a ledger sheet. We pitied them for their uselessness, barely tolerated their parasitic existence except as an occasional source of amusement. And now, alas, my son, we are the slaves of their mindless mood swings and their irrational whims. And we must pull the shades and huddle in our basements to practice our proud profession.

"In the days when they took me away and herded me and my fellow professionals into a kind of outdoor corral, where we were expected to pitch tents and fend for ourselves, the lawyers drew up secret contracts and the M.D.s kept in practice by breaking each other's arms and legs and resetting them in casts with the plaster with which we were supposed to sculpt. Imagine our horror when a conceptual artist caught a surgeon in the act one day and proceeded to sever one of those re-set limbs, seize it, and put it on display as art. We accountants set ourselves the arduous task of covertly recording debits and credits, balancing the books, as we used to say, for the day of reckoning. In their devilish perversion, knowing full well our intent, the artists provided ledgers free of charge and yet offered no remuneration for our endless labors and thus no incentive to proceed. And so we were obliged, just to stay in practice, to tap that dread exponential value they call the imagination, multiplying and dividing fictive figures with no bearing on any account.

"You can put two and two together. In a matter of weeks we were as scatterbrained as our keepers, and within a few months, elaborate doodles began appearing in our records. Some aberrant accountants even took liberties with the shape of numbers, so that in the end our ledgers proved as useless as a work of art. And then they established compulsory art education classes for our children, and were it not for our nightly lessons, I am afraid that you too, dear Albert, would have succumbed."

"No, father, never!" I cried.

"Your mother, a conscientious corporate climber whose mind was perfectly sound, I assure you (until she lost it and ran off with a knife thrower) made me swear nonetheless to continue your nightly lessons, but now my hours are numbered. It is up to you to practice and pass on what I have taught you. You must put on a convincing act in public, pretend to improvise, attend their premieres religiously, never miss an art opening and take pains not to fall asleep and snore at their interminable readings and recitals. But always, my son, when silence permits, train your mind to blot out the terrible thing they call imagination, and repeat the blessed $2 + 2 = 4$. Then proceed to run through the multiplication table, and while applauding the hysterical harangues and obscene gesticulations of their theatrical performances, count the claps and keep a tally in a hidden alcove of your mind.

"Someday our kind will return to prominence. And the calculator, that sacrosanct device they have reduced to a toy, will once again rule our lives. In the meantime, tally your breaths, count your heartbeats, and remember: Life is a balance sheet of profit and loss!"

These were my father's dying words. I buried him along with his beloved calculator and his neatly kept ledger. And I have tried my best to uphold his credo. Every night when the curtain of darkness falls on the day's dress rehearsal, I hurry home to huddle with my wife and children behind closed doors and direct the solemn recitation of the multiplication table: $2 \times 2 = 4$, $4 \times 4 = 16$, etc. But the effort seems ever more futile. Can my wife, an acrobat's daughter, really fathom the profound significance of ciphers? Do my children really care? Though I try to keep my mind on my calculations, my thoughts wander, and—dear father, forgive me!—I imagine a celestial registry, and there in a sandbox shoveling buckets of star dust, you sit, impeccable as ever in your pin-striped, three-piece suit, turning each bucket over and counting the cloud cakes. You smile at me and I smile too, trying to hold back the tears. But soon the image fades, however much I try to cling to it. And then at that bleak hour I must concede to a terrible uncertainty: Am I the secret accountant I pretend to be, or a shrewd imposter impersonating myself? Will posterity credit my balanced account as a faithful record of what once was or misconstrue it as a counterfeit, a hoax—or worse, a work of art?

Miracle at Mount Moriah

"...press 3 for directions, press 4 for cremation, press 5 for perpetual care."

Mount Moriah is, depending on your vantage point, a prime development with definite growth potential or the vestige of a lavish bygone real estate boom gone bust smack dab in the middle of the Borough of Queens. Implied palaces loom like the ruins of unrealized or faded dreams. Grandiose portals, their rusted iron gates ajar, affixed with noble bronze lions, dangling chains, ornately carved name plates and the like, all lead to the great unknown. And as in the cramped confines of a medieval hamlet huddled up against the castle wall, scattered rows of single-, double-occupancy and family plots marked for construction or demolition lie in a tight cluster. Here and there a stately Lilliputian villa rises like a toy palace out of the weeds and rubble. With real estate at such a premium, it's a wonder nobody has discovered the neighborhood. Or have they?

On a raw and rainy afternoon in late November, with winter already nipping at his heels, a homeless man of

hefty girth made himself at home in one such uninhab-
ited abode. His last flop had been in the now defunct
RKO Keith's Theatre, a once majestic movie palace at the
intersection of Northern Boulevard and Main Street, in
Flushing, into which he had managed to slip unnoticed
and curl up on the balcony. But just as Claude Rains
re-materialized on the silver screen at the end of the fifth
and final screening of *The Invisible Man*, so too was the
homeless man rooted out in the rude beam of a flashlight,
promptly expelled and forced to look for other lodgings.

The chapel door had been pried open by previous
visitors.

"Anybody home?" he asked.

No reply.

Aside from the brass candelabra, lions and other obscure
bric-a-brac inscribed with indecipherable lettering,
there also happened to be a very inviting looking bench.
Removing and hanging up several drenched layers of
clothing all the way down to his birthday suit, he stretched
himself out in right stately repose, a king in his castle. It
felt good to be horizontal and dry with the rain beating
on the roof. He lit a fire of ivy twigs and dried leaves he
found lying about, covered himself with the least damp
of his layers, a mildewy navy blue West Point cadet's cape
recently acquired at the Salvation Army, and promptly fell
asleep.

He dreamt he was a drifter in some strange city stretched
out asleep on the lower level of a parked double-decker

bus that rattled into spontaneous transit. "Step lively," the conductor, a talking caterpillar, cried, "the early bird catches the worm!" The drifter rolled under a seat just in time to avert the savage fangs of a flock of perfumed furies clambering aboard.

Oh the spiked heels! Oh the red toenails of morning!

Now the bus became a freight elevator. A rat scurried by. Or was it a blind boy? The blind rat-boy threw karate kicks in all directions. Then a family of human-spiders followed, mistaking him for a fly. Families can always sniff out a stranger in their midst, whatever the species. Frozen with terror, he was trapped, caught fast in the viscous snare of their love.

Awakened by the roar of a jet plane overhead, bright light streaming in through the stained glass window in the wake of the storm, the homeless man squinted, only now noticing an oddly misshapen baby doll on the bench beside him. Countless hands had done unspeakable things to the doll, with knives, with wires, with matches and explosives. Its eyes were pierced through, its hair ripped out, its lips and ears blown off. Yet what was left of its mangled face retained the hint of a sweet expression. Lying perfectly still, the homeless man suddenly became aware of someone else fondling the doll, half moaning, half chanting "Be My Baby" by the Ronettes.

—"What's that!?" A hand touched the intruder's toes.

—"Can't see ya, but ah sure can smell ya, boy!" The words were followed by the flick of a blade. Trembling, the homeless man felt fingers slide swiftly under the cape and grab hold of his private parts.

—"Make a move and y'ain't nevah goin' ta play nick-nack with yo' paddywack no more!" The homeless man gulped. "Now that we's come to an understandin'," said the voice belonging to the hand, "tell me what the hell you doin' in Blind Bertha's boudoir!"

"Bu...bu...bu...bu...bu," the homeless man blubbered, unable to shape words.

"Speak up, son!" Bertha urged, a cold metal blade sliding smoothly between the hairy hemispheres of his bare bottom, tilting ever so slightly like a knife on white bread, shaving off a few stray hairs. Twisting his head and straining his eyes, the homeless man gasped at the sight of massive thighs towering over him like the twin trunks of a pair of intertwined trees with bulbous fruits ripe unto bursting straining the hold of a flowery sarong.

"My my, they sho' is a lot of you, boy!" she said, feeling him all over. Bedecked with dark glasses and the bottom-less smile of the blind, Bertha spread terror and desire indiscriminately like peanut butter and jelly. The bewildered man responded with an explosion below.

"Cat got yer tongue, but ya sure can blow that horn!" Bertha laughed. "Now listen up, honky butt, 'n ya betta listen good, 'cause Bertha ain't goin' to say it twice! I can tell you's white from the smell o' yo' tail wind. Don't know what you up to, but you'd best get yo' white ass out'a here fast 'fore the Seven Dwarfs get back, else they goin' ta slice you up twelve ways to Christmas like a loaf of Wonder Bread, and th'ain't no glue gonna stick Ol' Humpy Dumpy back together again!...Shush up now! Too late! I hear 'em comin'!" she whispered, keeping a tight grip on his goods. "The boys's back!" She relaxed her grip to prove that she meant him no immediate harm. "Better play dead, son, less you wan' yo' private property subdivided."

Thinking fast, Bertha pulled the cape over the homeless man's head by way of a shroud. Through a rent, he glimpsed what followed.

Displaced gravel, a rusty squeaking hinge, cursing and belching heralded the arrival of the Seven Dwarfs, an integrated teenage gang, whose clubhouse he happened to have crashed.

—"Hey Bertha, since when you into stiffs!?"

—"Business be bad, Doc. The gravediggers gets it for free. So I does me a little freelance embalmin' on the side, ya know, just ta make ends meet."

—"That one sure as hell didn't die of starvation!"

Hearing the crinkle of paper,—"What ya got in the bag, Doc?" Bertha shrewdly changed the subject. "I ain't et since morning."

—"Abra cadabra!" Doc pulled a squirming, yelping mongrel puppy by its tail out of a brown paper bag.

—"So sweet o' you, boys, to think of me in my lonesome. I could use me a li'l house pet!"

Still yelping and squirming, the puppy tried to bite the

hand that held it.

"Damn, this bitch needs a fix!" said Doc.

The Seven Dwarfs all giggled as one. Bertha obliged with a smile. The homeless man held his breath.

—"Here, Dopey!" Doc passed the pup to a confederate while he dished out the goods. A little white powder on a spoon, a little flame from a Zippo lighter, a needle to suck it up and shoot.—"Hold the mutt still!" As the tip of the needle sank into the furry flesh, its little hind legs quivered.

—"Get down, doggy!"

Dopey dropped the pup. Somebody turned on a radio. The boys all laughed as they watched the mongrel puppy boogie.

"What kind is it, Doc?" asked Bertha, doing her best to keep the crew distracted.

"What kind o' what?" said Doc.

—"What kind o' dog?"

"Looks like a *hot* dog to me!" Doc snickered.

Everybody cracked up this time, including Bertha.

"Hey Sleepy," said Doc, "ever hump a dog!?"

Sleepy guffawed:—"Long as she got the buns, I got the mustard!"

Whereupon a curious sound emanated inopportunely from the sham corpse's posterior.

Doc eyed the stiff suspiciously, clasping the syringe, the contents of which he hadn't fully emptied into the puppy.—"What he die of, bean poisoning?"

"Cadavers leak!" said Bertha. "Ain't you never heard a dead man break wind before!?"

"Boys," said Doc, "get ready!"

"Christ, Doc!" replied Dopey, perplexed and expectant.

Doc waved the needle like a magic wand:—"Watch me make the dead rise! Bottom's up!" he snickered and stuck it to him.

Whereupon the corpse let out a colossal howl, Blind Bertha still holding tight to his now stiffly extended goods that made the cape rise.

"Holy shit, Doc," cried an incredulous Dopey, "you made the dead rise, it's a goddamn miracle!"

Doc had his doubts. Oh ye of little faith!

But just when things were about to get sticky for our latter day Lazarus, he was granted a reprieve from further indignities by the sacred sound of prayer.

—"*BARUCH OOVARUCH SHEMOH*!"

"Quick, Doc!" cried Sneezy, a breathless confederate stationed outside. "The Rabbis are coming!" And disinclined to blow their cover, the Seven Dwarfs made themselves scarce at the approach of two white bearded men in black suits and black hats.

—"Rebbe, I *tink* somebody's been tampering with the

tomb!"

—"Nonsense, Shimmy, who would dare intrude on the resting place of my in-laws of sainted memory!?"

—"With all due respect, Rebbe, I have learned never to say never."

—"You will remember, Shimmy, what the *Besht* said to the *Maggid*: 'My horses do not eat matzoth!'"

—"Forgive me, Rebbe, but to cite the *Aboth*: 'Whosoever has three qualities is of the disciples of Abraham, our father: a good eye, a humble mind, and a lowly spirit.' Of these, alas, I have only the first, but if ever it fails the service of my Lord, let Him pluck it out!"

"'Eye and heart,' says Reb Levi 'are the two go-betweens of sin,'" the Rebbe reminded with an ever so slightly sarcastic edge.

To which the other man replied: "'If thou give me thy heart and thine eyes, then I know that thou art mine.' Blessed be He, who hath taught me obedient blindness!" Whereupon he unlocked the door and beckoned for his master to precede him.

"HEAVEN FORBID!" The Rebbe fell into a faint upon entering the chapel.

Shimmy followed, hardly believing his eyes. Naked underneath their shrouds, their faces hidden from view, two Dybbuks of mighty proportions, a male and a female, impersonating the Rebbe's deceased *machatenista*, his in-laws of blessed memory, squirmed, one on top of the other, their legs obscenely intertwined.—"This I witnessed with mine own two eyes—may the Lord pluck them out if I lie!" he swore, before likewise falling into a swoon.

The dead, as a class, are non-judgmental by nature. You can lie beside them, above them, among them, and they will take you as you are.

Not so the living.

Blind Bertha absconded with the cape, considering it fair recompense.

Abandoned, shaken to the core, the homeless man pulled on the layers of clothing he had left and set off in search of breakfast. A crumpled scrap of paper flapping from the leafless branch of a tree caught his eye. He plucked it from the branch and read:

"From the Land of Miracles comes
COUNTESS MARVELLA
and she says:
DON'T GIVE UP!
GUARANTEED RESULTS IN 24 HOURS
THIS CONTINENTAL BORN SPIRITUALIST
who
BRINGS YOU
the solutions to the mysteries of life,
seeks to help many thousands, like yourself, who have been
CROSSED, HAVE SPELLS, CAN'T HOLD MONEY,
WANT LUCK, WANT THEIR LOVED ONES BACK,
WANT TO STOP NATURE'S PROBLEMS *or* WANT TO
GET RID OF STRANGE SICKNESS.

IF YOU REALLY WANT SOMETHING DONE
HERE IS THE WOMAN WHO WILL DO IT FOR YOU
IN A HURRY.
DON'T TELL HER. LET HER TELL YOU.
THIS WOMAN DOES WHAT OTHERS ONLY CLAIM
TO DO!!!!
DON'T WAIT FOR RELIEF!!!! CALL NOW!!!!!!!!!!!
ONE FREE QUESTION BY PHONE)

Spotting a public phone outside the cemetery office, lacking a quarter, he nevertheless felt driven to dial. Fate and faulty equipment were on his side.

—"Countess!"

—"Who!?"

—"The Countess Marvella, please!"

—"Oh yeah, hold it!...Countess Marvella here, how can she...I help you?"

—"I don't know."

—"Whiskey?"

—"No."

—"Gambling?"

—"No."

—"Impotence?"

—"I don't think so."

—"Inexplicable disturbance just happens to be my specialty!...Visa, Mastercard or American Express?"

Silence.

—"Money troubles too, huh!? Time is money! Why don't you come visit me in person during my office hours when you've got the wherewithal. The Lord provideth. I'll pass you to my secretary to make an appointment."

A pause.

Chimes rudely interrupted.—"DEPOSIT FIVE CENTS OR YOUR CALL WILL BE TERMINATED!"

"But I didn't get to ask my free question!" the homeless man bitterly complained to the wind of the electrical void. Feeling defeated, as usual, he replaced the receiver in its bed, when out poured a shower of quarters, Atlantic-City-slot-machine-style.

"Thank you, Countess Marvella! Thank you from the bottom of my heart!" he half-laughed, half-wept, rich enough for once to pay for a stack of pancakes, hot coffee and a flop. Feeling hopeful, despite the chill in the air, the homeless man headed straight for the International House of Pancakes, jingling the change in his pocket, unaware of the hole, preoccupied for the first time in a long while making plans. First he'd eat his fill. Then he'd stop by at the Salvation Army to replace his cape and see if they needed any Santas for Christmas.

Enoch Sapphire

Other than that he died and had a striking name, nothing else is known about Enoch Sapphire. So let us lend him a life.

Let us conjecture that there came a moment, when, unwed, childless, a solitary malcontent, realizing he had missed all the ordinary pleasures, Enoch stepped out of his cramped apartment, filled with furniture inherited from a maiden aunt—the same aunt who left him the modest trust fund that provided for his modest needs—and various and sundry nondescript possessions, including, likewise inherited from said aunt, a special subscription, deluxe, Moroccan red leather bound edition of the complete *Reader's Digest* from 1963 till 1987, when, for no particular reason, despite repeated reminders, he let the subscription lapse; never having exchanged so much as a nod with his neighbors on either side, he entered the freight elevator, the passenger elevator being out of service, intending to take it down to the lobby to go through the mechanical motions of yet another uneventful day, suddenly deciding instead to ride up to the roof, or rather, the floor directly beneath the roof; and indulging a squelched urge that he had harbored all his life, he shoved open the sticky, tar-papered door, and emerged, 37 flights above the street, where at that very moment he witnessed two pigeons coupling; and when, bending closer to study the physiology of aviary reproduction, with what appendages and what cavities they did it, failed to notice the loose rain gutter; and in the instant of his fall, a kaleidoscope of images broke through the gray shell he had come to accept as the inherent limitations of life, and in his heart welled up a long dormant longing that surged forth and fortuitously met, in a manner of speaking, a woman, a perfect stranger, with whom he was smitten and who he smote and promptly crushed.

This, you might rightfully assume, was the end of the story.

But wait, Enoch ached, badly mangled and maimed, yet eternally grateful to the lady lying beneath him whose body had muffled his fall.

"I owe you my life," he whispered, nostril to nostril.

He listened, but there was no heart beat. No, he resolved, fighting off temptation, it would be too crude to take liberties.

Heartbroken, his lips twitched a while till they fell still, locked into the semblance of a smile.

Leonard's Drip

Consider Leonard. A lad of dry temperament and thin lips, practically parched in affect and mind, dry as the desert. His dryness had always been a point of pride, till one day he began to drip. At first he thought it was the rain coming in through a leak in the ceiling of his modest mansard. But he looked out the window and saw that it was sunny, not a cloud in the sky. Then he thought it might be a problem with the pipes.

So Leonard called the plumber, but the plumber's assistant said the boss was busy at the moment, and to try again tomorrow.

"It's a bad drip," said Leonard.

"A bucket might be advisable as a stop-gap measure," replied the assistant.

So Leonard fetched a rain bucket, actually a cracked crock pot that doubled as a bucket to catch leaks in inclement weather, and placed it strategically where he had last detected the suspicious moisture. But when he moved about the mansard—actually an attic, though being a bit old-fashioned and somewhat stuck-up, Leonard preferred to refer to it as a mansard—the dripping followed him like a lapdog. It was then that he noticed upon turning about, a telltale trail of droplets gathered in his wake.

Alarmed, Leonard bent down to inspect the liquid. Relieved at least to find that it was not red, as he feared, he was nevertheless concerned to confirm without a doubt that the drip did not emanate from his immediate surroundings, neither from ceiling, windows, walls nor floor, but from what seemed rather to come from somewhere inside himself.

A fretful Leonard called the doctor. "I'm dripping," he said to the doctor's secretary.

"I'm sorry to hear that," she said, "the doctor can see you next Wednesday."

"Can't he make it any sooner?"

"Wednesday," she said.

"Very well," said Leonard, now positively distraught, and hung up.

Wednesday was a full five days away, and meanwhile the desperate lad had to deal with his drip.

He bent down, brought his nose close to sniff the clear concavity, observing that the drip had no noticeable odor, and consequently could not possibly have emanated from either the anterior or the posterior. Perhaps it's perspiration, he thought. Never having invested in an air conditioner, let alone a fan—not so much out of parsimony, though he had indeed been called a tightwad, among other things, by his erstwhile fiancée, who left him for a dentist with sweaty palms and disposable income, but rather on account of a certain innate torpor, an inertia that made decisions difficult—whatever the weather, Leonard had for as long as he could remember always remained dry.

Must be global warming, he pondered, a climactic condition adamantly denied by his next door neighbor, Mr. Moskowitz, who kept an American flag flapping outside his window at all times, an amalgam of skepticism and faith, science and taxes be damned. Leonard kept his own tabs on the weather by means of a Centigrade thermometer made in Thailand he had once, to please his faithless paramour, attached to his own window frame, though he was unable to convert Centigrade to Fahrenheit—which device, he suddenly fathomed with a start, was itself a glass-enclosed drip. A mere droplet of mercury can be deadly if ever it seeped out; he shuddered at the prospect, pulled down the shade and huddled in terror.

Perhaps, he thought, I have always dripped, and just never noticed it till now. Yes, it must be so, he tried to think back, but try as he might he could not remember any undue moisture or condensation ever gathering either on his lip or brow or in his wake. He had always remained dry. With no other recourse, given the fact that it was five days until the doctor could see him, Leonard decided to study the residue.

With a cracked wooden ruler preserved from childhood, from which most of the numbers had been effaced, he tried to measure the diameter of each drop. Two centimeters across, he estimated. Hesitating at first, his curiosity got the better of his alarm, and he went so far as to first finger, and then graze the surface of one of the telltale drops with his tongue, thinking that perhaps it might be tears. I must be sad, he thought. But the drop was not salty. Now what?

He searched his body for blisters that might have burst and oozed, but found none.

He dropped his pants and patted first his boxer fly then his bottom. Dry. He raised his shirt and twisted his neck to examine his back as best he could in a tall mirror he'd tacked to the closet door, another concession to his former attachment, which for sentimentality's sake and the afore-mentioned torpor, he couldn't quite bring himself to remove when she left him for the dentist. Then he remembered his nose, the only part of him that occasionally dribbled in cold weather, but it too was dry. He scratched his itchy scalp, producing a veritable avalanche of dandruff flakes. But in all these investigations he came up high and dry.

He had read somewhere that the human body was 57 percent water, 75 percent in newborns, and peering at himself in the mirror, felt a bit like a leaky lake or a water balloon of the sort he had once flung out the window on a hapless passerby as a prank in adolescence. Is Man then nothing but a leaky water balloon? he pondered. But being dry-minded and practical, he immediately blotted out such metaphysical musings.

Everyone leaks at some point in his life, why it's perfectly natural, he told himself. Infants drip daily. Women leak monthly. The elderly are afflicted with a chronic drip. But being neither infant, nor female, nor as yet addled with age, his life had heretofore, as previously stated, been a long dry spell.

Does this mean that age is upon me? Leonard fretted, and decided to forestall the onset. Others dye their hair or get a face lift to turn back the clock. I'll plug up the drip, he resolved, whatever the source.

Stripping naked, standing now with his back to the tall dressing mirror, and tilting every which way a small round powder mirror he'd one day on a whim filched from his ex's purse and kept stashed away as a sort of subliminal souvenir, he strained to peruse the otherwise hidden sectors of self. But try as he might, he found no swollen pore, no bruise, no bulge, no blister.

That night he went to bed wearing an adult diaper to test for possible incontinence, but awakened dry below. Relieved, having all but forgotten the source of his concern, Leonard leaned out of bed and looked down to find his face reflected in a little circle of droplets.

He leapt out of bed in a panic. Get a handle on yourself, Leonard! he commanded, and contrary to his ordinary stasis, decided to get dressed and go for a walk, with the ulterior, albeit unspoken, motive of testing whether the drip would follow, or whether it was strictly domestic.

His drip, alas, went with him.

Embarrassed, lest the world become aware of his leak, he decided to follow a man walking his golden retriever. Leonard watched from a distance as the canine, a male, stopped periodically, lifting his hind leg to spray and sniff the trail of dried up residual sprays. It was a handsome dog with a golden coat of fur, and the owner was rightfully proud of his pet. After a while he sat down on a bench, and it being sunny out, promptly fell asleep with a contented smile. Leonard envied the man for his evident contentment and for having such a fine pet. It was then, as if cognizant of his unspoken longings, that the dog came over to sniff at him. Not long enough to allow for such canine license, the leash slipped from the sleeping man's hand.

"Get lost!" said Leonard, embarrassed, trying to shoo it away with the toe of his loafer.

But the dog was determined and sniffed him all over, taking evident delight in his drip. Leonard was mortified, paralyzed with shame, lest people notice. But when the dog proceeded, first to sniff, then to lick up the trail of telltale drops, Leonard had an idea.

Looking around to make sure that the master was still asleep, and that no one else noticed, Leonard grabbed hold of the leash, took a few exploratory steps and kept walking. It was his intention to employ the creature as a foil, to blame it for his leak. Just as he had hoped, instead of walking ahead, as dogs are wont, it trailed behind, first sniffing then licking up his drops.

Leonard took the dog home with him. He resolved to return to the bench the next day and leave an envelope addressed to "The Man Who Lost his Retriever" stuffed with a wad of bills commensurate with the dog's value.

Having found, if not the source of the problem, at least a solution to his dilemma, the perfect antidote, a walking mop to wipe up the trace of his leaky self, Leonard was well pleased.

But pets were not permitted in the building in which he lived. And wouldn't you know it—Leonard suspected Moskowitz—the next day the super came by and told him the dog would have to go.

Distraught as he was, Leonard resolved to return the animal to its master.

He spotted the man in the distance, seated on the same bench on which he had seen him the day before, looking forlorn. Careful not to be noticed, Leonard dodged with the retriever behind a tree. Uncharacteristically swift and decisive, he let go of the leash, and watched from behind the trunk as the dog ran to his master. Overjoyed, the man hugged the dog. The dog licked the man's face.

"Where have you been, boy?"

The dog barked.

The man looked around to see where he came from.

But Leonard had meanwhile dodged behind a nanny wheeling a baby carriage, holding a toddler by the hand. The toddler paused and tugged at the nanny's hand. The nanny scowled. Leonard noticed the trail of drops.

"I told you to go before we went out!" she scolded.

Briefly, very briefly, he contemplated kidnapping the child as an alternate foil, but that would be going too far.

Leonard sighed, relieved to come to his senses, deciding henceforth to make do with his drip, to accept it as one might baldness, a limp or a stutter, or some other impediment. He decided to buy a lemon Italian ice to celebrate his newfound resolve.

"It's no-drip ice," said the ice cream vendor.

"Come again?" said Leonard.

"To keep the kiddies clean," the vendor replied.

Leonard paid and slunk off in shame, lest the vendor notice his drip.

When he got home he set the ice on the window sill where most people keep potted plants.

And wonder of wonders, it not only refrained from dripping, but spread its influence on its surroundings. Rather than melt, it sucked up all moisture in its immediate periphery.

All day Leonard sat admiring the ice, unique as it was, identifying with it in some wordless way as the embodiment of his former dryness. For the longest time he was well pleased, and then—funny the way the mind works, craving back what it once reviled—and reflecting on a dryness he had always taken for granted, Leonard missed the drip. In a fit of indecipherable emotions he hurled the dry lemon ice out the window just as Moskowitz was getting home from work. Leonard shrank back out of sight, chuckling to himself as Moskowitz wiped the residue from his bald pate.

"Damn pigeons!" Moskowitz cursed.

Leonard turned on the T.V. The weatherman predicted rain.

Fly, a Fable

However did the fly get in? The windows were shut tight, the air-conditioner on high cool. It would have had to brave the whirling blades and slip through the coolant and filter. Impossible! There must be a minuscule chink in the wall or a crack between window and frame, an invisible point of entry through which this noisome emissary of the outside penetrated all defenses.

Never underestimate the versatility of a fly, its ability to infiltrate vaults and virtual vacuums, its acrobatic prowess. The most graceful bird is a klutz in comparison. A fly can perform astounding whirligigs in thin air, taunting us all the while with its brazen buzz, crawl straight up sheer verticals and hang upside-down above us with utter disdain, silently laughing it seems. "Looking at flies in terms of weight to volume, they don't weigh much, so very little force is required to keep a fly from falling," according to Dr. Alex Mintzer, of the Entomological Society of America, in Lanham, Maryland.

Flies have inspired extravagant verbal flights of fancy. English has its "Spanish fly" and "a fly in the ointment." The Germans have their fairy tale of "The Brave Little Tailor" able to fell seven in a single blow—flies, that is.

But the French take the cake with the vinegary Gallic argot insult *"enculeur de mouches!"* something like an Anglo-Saxon nit-picker, though the literal translation (fly sodomite) defies the imagination.

I was once so lonely I befriended a fly. Fed it. Tried to teach it tricks. Let it land on me where it pleased and scurry down naked limbs, I refrained from bathing for its sake and let it languish in sweaty dipterous erogenous zones. It was an ordinary red-headed housefly, nothing exotic, but I liked to watch it rub its hind legs gleefully and turn in a frenzy. On one occasion while admiring its wild St. Vitus dance I noticed with an adrenal rush that its tail was the same color as its head. I waited three days and shed a tear before I killed it.

Nothing, but nothing, can spoil a good meal like insects hovering round your plate.

Here I was about to spear up a bleeding morsel of steak when a tiny winged moocher that somehow managed to gain access to my kitchen executed seven turns—I counted them—seven turns around my head by way of choreographed prowl before boldly landing with devilish precision on the crest of the very slab I ogled with salivating longing. (In Medieval iconography, the fly is a symbol of the Devil, and I am inclined to concur with the sentiment that inspired the symbol.)

Picture my state!

I swiped at it with my checkered red serviette, but the insolent insect toyed with the cloth like a brave bull, standing its ground, returning after each swipe to the same spot, bathing its bandy little legs in the juice on my plate.

Then a curious thing happened.

Anger fused with hunger, spiked with a sudden spell of perfect concentration, settling into the studied calm of a micro-matador.

And guided by a pure act of will, I lowered the knife, distracting my victim with my red checkered *muletta*, intending to deliver the death blow, but instead, felled the fly, split it down the middle, severing it precisely in two.

Stunned by the force of the stroke, itself as yet oblivious to the fact of having been halved, and still entertaining the illusion of unity, it continued to kick its separate sets of legs in a futile frenzy before succumbing to its divided state.

My appetite intact, aroused all the more by the hunger-enhancing thrill of victory, I brushed aside the fallen wings and finished off my dinner.

Barking Love

The story was a farewell gift, though I didn't realize it at the time. We lived in the same building, a faceless high-rise, I on the 12th floor, she on the 13th; we'd met in the elevator, she having caught me furtively flipping through a dog-eared paperback copy of *Lolita* and remarked in passing that Vladimir, the lewd rascal, had been an old acquaintance. One word led to another. So began our friendship. Once a week I brought her dinner; watered the palm tree she kept in a pot, summers outside on the terrace, winters in the tropical warmth of the living room; poured us both red wine from a big bottle that never seemed to run dry; and we let our words wander where they wanted, although mostly I just sat by in silence and lent her a listening ear.

At the time she was already 93 years old, and I almost half a century younger. Her gaunt, shriveled figure with a messy head of formerly blond, now chalky white, hair was hardly alluring; but looking deep into her sparkling blue eyes and listening to the lively melody of her voice, you could still unearth the traces of a wizened beauty in the ruins of age, and well imagine, as she herself proudly confessed, that in years gone by she could attract men and women, never mind the sex, like flies to a burning fire. Once when it was hot and she impatiently peeled off the baggy gray sweater, her favorite piece of clothing, she let the nipple of a withered breast peek out, carelessly no doubt, but when she realized what she'd done, she flashed me a sly smile and shrugged her shoulders, testing the effect for the blink of an eye, before grinning and shoving the breast back under the blouse. We drank, sometimes smoked, and talked of books, hers and those of others. Old age, she said, was a curse. She lacked the force in her arthritic fingers to pound on her old Olivetti and the concentration to squeeze novels out of life. But the desire to communicate was still strong.

A dog barked outside.

"The dog did not belong to me," she began. "Even as a young child I had an aversion to tamed animals. I whirled cats around by their tails and flung them from the balcony out into the street. Dogs were too heavy, I just chased them out of the house. 'You are an unnatural child,' my mother said. 'Naturally!' I replied with an insolent grin."

"But you tolerate palm trees."

"Because they're self-sufficient!"

"Indeed," I replied, "when someone else waters them!"

Whereupon she nodded, noticeably annoyed. The story was already underway and Madame could not abide interruptions.

"The dog belonged to my lover of the moment, a

Ukrainian sailor with the Merchant Marines. Don't ask me what kind of dog it was. He was big and dark brown with white spots in the face and a muzzle full of sharp teeth that didn't frighten me, since he turned his rage on the sailor. It was a bad neighborhood, the barking frightened off burglars, so the man tolerated the animal's angry fits. The sailor spoke next to no English and I not a word of Ukrainian. He himself barked out a word or two every now and then. 'Come!... Me want!... Good!... Enough!...' Sometimes I thought he'd learned to communicate from the dog that wagged his tail in an understanding manner and barked back. The sailor and I spent little time together, and that mostly only in the dark, where in any case words don't really matter. And since he was often at sea, I had to take care of the dog in his absence.

"I soon grew accustomed to his barking, even managed to decipher what he wanted—hunger, thirst, the need to relieve himself outside—I understood him much better than I did the sailor, who mostly just grabbed for what he wanted. Like I said, he was often at sea. In the morning when I sat stooped over my Olivetti, the dog lay at my feet and only seldom bothered me when the need grew overwhelming. One time to my great amazement, I noticed that he even tried to mimic my fingers, striking out the rhythm of my typing with his tail, and when I hesitated, searching for the right word, he groaned quietly, as if he wanted to reassure me: 'Don't get so upset, it'll come to you, don't worry!'

"In fact, the dog and I got along a lot better than either

of us did with the sailor, upon whose return there was always a scene. As soon as he touched me the dog barked loudly and the sailor struck him in the snout. 'Woman mine!' the man barked back and the dog bared his teeth. And when the sailor wanted to satisfy his need with me, he first had to take the dog into the bathroom and tie him to the shower, where he kept right on barking. The neighbors complained. The Yugoslav super, who didn't speak much English either, slipped a note under the door: 'Dog go!' I defended the poor creature, and come night, as soon as the sailor was snoring, I slipped off to the bathroom, where I petted him on the head, behind the ears, on the belly and sometimes even below where man and dog are alike. The barking faded into a satisfied groan.

"One evening the sailor came home dead drunk. He'd already spent a month straight on dry land and he'd had enough. But since he was unable to express his displeasure, vodka was the only available remedy. I think maybe the drinking helped him to dissolve the oppressive inflexibility of the hard ground, and to float like a whale in the waves with the fluid illusion of freedom. I had long tolerated his moods. He was a big, handsome man with strong arms, the left tattooed with a naked mermaid, and watery ocean-blue eyes in the wild waves of which I happily drowned. One can forgive a lot to beauty. But this time he repelled me, like a slobbering creature from the deep.

"'Fuck!' he barked his crude intention.

"'Tired!' I muttered, shaking my head.

"He grabbed me by the hair and dragged me from the table where I sat, with the dog at my feet, over to the bed.

"He tore the clothes from my body. There was nothing I could do to stop him. I lay there under his weight, trembling with fear and cold, and waited for the storm waves to billow themselves out.

"But this time he'd forgotten to tie the animal to the shower. And as he mounted me, the dog bounded onto his back and bit him in the thigh. The sailor groaned, confused in his alcoholic stupor between pleasure and pain; he turned around to strike the dog, but the animal was faster and bit the man in the arm. Howling, bleeding and barking with pain and rage, the sailor staggered out of bed, tore open the door and plodded down the stairs.

"I lay there in bed, my heart beating, my body dabbed with blood. The dog lay beside me, his nostrils quivering, and licked the bloodstains from my breast and legs. I must admit that, aside from fear and cold, I also felt something else, cravings that I ordinarily stilled with strangers in the dark. Now the dog and I looked at each other. We were no strangers. My mother always said I was unnatural, but is there anything more natural…or what do you think?"

Stunned, I said nothing.

"You surely must know the story by Balzac," she added.

"The one about the soldier and the lioness in the desert?"

"It was a panther…a beautiful beast."

"But that was just a story."

She grinned. "The Russian Empress Catherine the Great is said to have had a thing for thoroughbred Arabian steeds."

I never knew with her if she meant something seriously or just wanted to test my reaction. She took an immense pleasure in saying scandalous things, appropriating to old age the privilege of youth.

"And the sailor?" I asked.

"Good riddance!" she underlined, with a sneer, the irrelevance of the question. Whereupon she paused. "But with the dog, that was true love…which I think back to, greatly stirred, every time I hear barking."

It was our next to last conversation.

We did not see each other for quite a while after that. I confess that I was taken aback by the story.

Her friends threw her a party for her 95th birthday, to which I too was invited. But she was no longer altogether there.

I brought her flowers. "Where's the palm tree?" I searched for it in vain.

She looked at me, tried to situate the face in the muddle of memories. "I know that you're somebody, but I don't remember who."

Torn by sadness, I flung myself at her feet, bowed my head and started barking.

Outside a dog barked back.

All conversations suddenly stopped. Even among artists and writers there are certain boundaries of decorum. The other guests did not know whether to burst out laughing or to fetch me a straitjacket.

But she searched my face with a fleeting flicker of recognition.

The Fairy Tale of the Blessed Meal

The following tale was told in the Concentration Camp Hoffnungslos. One day SS-Unterscharführer Haselbeck, a man who seldom took notice of the world around him, was very surprised to observe that the prisoners in his block licked their fingers every time they dipped them into their miserable slop.

„Jews, Monkeys, and Freemasons have no taste," he muttered half-loud to himself.

Whereupon a voice whispered in his ear: „Blessed meal!"

In his childhood, before he joined the Party, he was raised in a pious home. Every evening his mother told him: „The Lord God thinks of you even if you don't think of Him."

Haselbeck shook his head to clear his thoughts.

But since the finger licking kept repeating itself, the Unterscharführer became curious. So he asked the prisoner in charge: „Why do you dirty Jews lick your filthy fingers?"

„Because the food tastes good, Herr Unterscharführer,"
the latter replied.

Which really pricked his curiosity. Since the prisoners
were given nothing but miserable shreds of meat and bones
you wouldn't give a dog, rotten cabbage and potatoes.
In school Haselbeck had learned that Jews are sly and
practice black magic. The Jew can turn dung into gold, the
teacher said.

So Haselbeck hid behind a giant kettle the morning of
the weekly delivery of foodstuffs, from which he always
siphoned off his share to sell back to the sons of bitches,
since every Jew has a secret stock of money and valuables
which he hides up his ass or in some other place for
safekeeping. The provender and perishables were taken in
by a little man with delicate features and a long nose, who
sniffed everything over like a dog and politely thanked
the prisoners in the delivery detail. And once the others
were gone and the little man reached for the giant kettle,
the Unterscharführer slipped behind an even bigger vat.
He looked on with amazement as the curious little man
carefully sorted everything, severed the maggoty parts of
the meat and mildewed vegetables with the dull blade of
a broken pocket knife, and rowed the rest in even little
heaps on a broken cutting board. From each pants pocket
he then pulled out a handful of weed and lay it beside the
foodstuffs on the board.

And when the little man reached for the kettle and the
Unterscharführer had nowhere else to hide, he leapt forth

and said: „I caught you, you sly devil. What kind of black magic are you plotting with your weed? Who do you plan to poison?"

A bit taken aback, but keeping his composure, the little man smiled: „That is no black magic, Herr Unterscharführer, Sir. I was a cook at the Hotel Adlon!"

„And what kind of foul weed is that you dumped in your brew?"

„There are wild herbs growing in the outlying fields around the camp. I ask the prisoners engaged in the work details outside the camp perimeter to gather them for me."

Now the Unterscharführer, who had never set foot, and surely not his nose, in a fancy restaurant, looked on as the little man chopped up meat and vegetables and dropped them into sizzling margarine in the kettle, poured water in after a while, rubbed the dry herbs between the palms of his hands so that the crushed leaves fell in and only the branches were left, whereupon he brought it all to a boil. And time and again he dipped his spoon in to taste, until finally he was satisfied.

„Would you like to taste a spoonful, Herr Unterscharführer, Sir?" he asked Haselbeck.

Frightened at first, the SS-Man held back. That chiseler surely wants to poison me, he thought. But when he saw the little man lick his spoon clean with delight, he pulled his service spoon out of his pocket, dipped it in gingerly to have a little taste, and could not believe his tongue. The stuff was so good, he dipped his spoon in again, this time deep down, and fetched himself a heaping spoonful.

„This is really delicious !" he said to the little man. „Much better than the slop they feed us in the mess hall."

„Glad to hear it," the cook smiled back.

Such a secret the Unterscharführer initially resolved to keep to himself to turn to his account later. Every week Haselbeck was at hand at the scheduled delivery time to oversee receipt of the stock, and came back when it was done to relish the result.

One day Haselbeck heard that the Commandant's wife wished to prepare a Christmas meal like in the good old days, but that her young Polish cook was pregnant, liable to give birth any day now, and consequently not in any condition to whip up a proper holiday spread. Whereupon Unterscharführer Haselbeck stepped forward and said: „Dear Madame Commandant, I know a cook who can perform wonders in the kitchen."

„Have him brought to me!" the woman replied, overjoyed.

Naturally Unterscharführer Haselbeck did not dare confess to the Commandant's wife that the cook in question was a prisoner—and a Jew to boot!

And the next time he visited the cook at the scheduled delivery time in the prisoner's kitchen, he brought him a suit of clothes he'd filched from the clothing repository of the new arrivals.

„Now go wash up so that you don't stink, and put

on a decent suit of clothes! You have an important appointment."

„But first I have to prepare food for the prisoners, Herr Unterscharführer, Sir! Duty is duty!" the little man protested.

„The dirty dogs can wait for their slop!" Haselbeck screamed.

„At your service, Herr Unterscharführer." the prisoner replied.

So the SS-Man looked around to make sure nobody noticed and took the disguised prisoner with him to visit the Commandant's wife.

„Speak only when you're spoken to. Don't let slip that you're a prisoner, and for heaven's sake not that you're a Jew. Or else there'll be trouble!"

So Unterscharführer Haselbeck introduced the little man to the Commandant's wife. She served him tea and cake. And after they'd discussed the weather for a while, and she'd inquired if he thought it was going to rain tomorrow, she sounded him out as to his favorite dish.

Whereupon he replied: „Smothered Goose Heaven and Earth Style."

„What an odd name for a dish," she remarked.

„That was the most popular main dish at Christmas-time in the great dining room of the Hotel Adlon. Back then I was a fledgling apprentice in the kitchen. I learned the art of cooking from the Chef de Cuisine, Monsieur

Délice, a Frenchman."

„Ah, the Hotel Adlon!" the woman sighed. „Once in childhood, my dear old grandpa took me there for coffee and cake. He pulled out his pipe, stroked his mustache and laughed with pleasure to see me lick up the last drops of my hot chocolate from the bottom of my cup. It was and remains a smoke-enveloped dream. – Smothered goose? Why not?" she replied, completely consumed by the memory. „But it has to taste particularly good! My husband works so hard. I want to lighten his load for an evening."

„It would be a great pleasure for me to fulfill your wish, dear lady."

So the SS-Man bid the prisoner prepare a list, and fetched him everything he needed. And on the day before Holy Night Unterscharführer Haselbeck brought the prisoner a white chef's coat and pants and a white toque. And the cook cooked up such a splendid feast Christmas Eve that the Commandant kept fluttering his eyebrows with pleasure and even licked his lips.

The next day the cook was requested to appear at the Commandant's office. The Unterscharführer was a bit concerned. It's one thing to put on a performance for the Commandant's wife and quite another to dare do so before the Commandant. But he had no choice. Once having instigated a lie, the truth could cost him incarceration or much worse.

„That will be all!" the Commandant commanded the

Unterscharführer, whereupon the Commandant reached out his hand to the disguised prisoner and politely inquired: „With whom have I the honor?"

Unterscharführer Haselbeck trembled as he peeked through the keyhole and overheard the following conversation.

„The name is Riesig."

The SS-Man had to smile, his upset notwithstanding. Strange name for a little Jewish rascal.

„You are a veritable wizard in the kitchen, Herr Riesig," the Commandant remarked. „I have a big favor to ask. I will soon receive a very important guest. Although it's a secret, I can tell you: It's Reichsführer Himmler. I would like you to cook something delicious for him, the only thing is he's a vegetarian!"

„No problem, Herr Commandant!" the cook replied. „I'll prepare my smothered goose heaven and earth style without the goose. Only I will need some very special herbs."

The Commandant bid the trembling Unterscharführer return and commanded him to: „Assemble a farming commando and have everything planted that Herr Riesig requires!"

Haselbeck followed orders. A field was planted with all sorts of herbs and vegetables.

Whereupon the little man said: „I will need a barnyard full of geese."

„Why geese? The Reichsführer is a vegetarian after all!" the Unterscharführer protested.

„The geese are only needed to produce the dung to enrich the herbs, potatoes and apples."

„What a shame to waste the goose flesh!" the Unterscharführer winked.

So Haselbeck had the prisoners build a barnyard and filled it with fat geese from Hungary.

The cackling of the geese disturbed the Commandant in his work. „The fowl must disappear at once!" he ordered the unnerved Unterscharführer.

„If you please, Herr Commandant, Sir, the cook needs the geese to prepare the meal for your important guest," the Unterscharführer replied.

„Dismantle the barnyard at once and move it to the camp. The racket is intolerable, it disturbs my concentration!"

„At once, Herr Commandant, Sir!" replied the Unterscharführer, who put together another commando to dismantle and rebuild it in the camp.

The prisoners' ration tasted better every day. Scents and rumors circulated around the entire camp.

Then came the day of the important visit. The little prisoner was once again dressed up as chef de cuisine and brought to a kitchen especially outfitted for the occasion by the Commandant to prepare the meal.

The following rumor circulated: Reichsführer Himmler

liked the appetizers well enough. But when he tasted the main dish, he almost fainted, he liked it so much he asked for a second serving.

„I want to meet the cook!" he ordered.

„At once, Herr Reichsführer," replied the joyous Commandant, who had the little man called in from the kitchen.

„My congratulations!" said the Reichsführer, his glasses all fogged up with the steam of the savory broth. „That was some meal. What is the main dish called?"

„Smothered goose heaven and earth style," said the prisoner.

At these words the important person almost choked. „Everybody knows that I am a vegetarian, like the Führer himself."

„The dung and the cackling merely help fortify the potatoes, apples and herbs, Herr Reichsführer."

„You look familiar to me. Where did you learn to cook?"

„In the Hotel Adlon before the war, my Führer," the prisoner replied.

Impressed, the Reichsführer asked for the recipe and for a package for the return trip to Berlin—what the Americans call a *doggy bag.*

„Gladly, my Führer!"

And what was in the doggy bag?

Goose droppings of course.

So they said in the KZ Hoffnungslos, where for a while the prisoners supped on goose stew. Not a living soul can confirm the truth of the rumor, and surely not a smothered goose.

And what became of the cook? Did he survive the camp?

After the War he is said to have run a small restaurant in Berlin. And one day the former Commandant, who had in the meantime become the director of a wholesale grain business, came to eat.

Was he not arrested and condemned?

There is no record of the KZ Hoffnungslos.

When the cook poked his head out of the kitchen and saw him enter the restaurant with his wife, he was anxious at first.

But when he saw the expression on the faces of his guests when they read „smothered goose heaven and earth style," on the menu, he smiled to himself.

The goose was ordered and served. The grain merchant poked around in his plate. But his wife, who had in the meantime put on considerable weight, furtively licked her fingers and was just gnawing on a bone, when the cook came out of the kitchen and introduced himself: „We know each other from before."

„Impossible!" muttered the stunned grain merchant.

„Indeed we do!" replied the cook and turned to the wife: „Greetings, dear lady!"

„Herr Riesig from the Hotel Adlon!" she smiled, a bit disconcerted.

„Klein from the KZ Hoffnungslos!" the cook corrected.

Whereupon the woman cackled, jerked her head back like a goose, and choked on the bone.

But fairytales are supposed to have a happy ending.

So what's not to be happy about?

The grain merchant went bankrupt. Klein took over the business.

And mankind, what did they learn from it all?

Not a thing.

But in the barnyard you can still hear to this very day a satisfied cackle.

The Shrinking Gardens

Two *shriveled paralytics in parallel beds tell each other tall tales to kill time.*

—"Once, when I still had the use of my limbs, the Sultana of Oman invited me to visit her famous shrinking gardens. 'Dear Sir,' the Sultana confessed, 'the sand which surrounds us and dominates the minuscule portion of eternity that Allah in his beneficence has accorded mankind allows us nevertheless to cultivate a garden. But the desert, fierce mother, devours what she gives. To survive, our trees have had to develop contracting roots. A cartographer of the 11th century drew a map of the oasis, measuring its surface in square camel's hooves. You'd need a high power electron microscope to spot a trace of it nowadays, though we believe it's still there.'"

—"Inflation," the listener interrupts (and would have nodded if he could). "My grandfather had a nose like a carrot, whereas my father's nose was downright modern, and mine—well, as you can tell, it's hardly worth wiping. Which reminds me of another story..."

The Thousand and Second Night

He was an Ethiopian prince and she the daughter of a wealthy widower, an Egyptian merchant, who, for reasons unknown, had settled in Vevey, Switzerland. They met one evening at a diplomats' ball. It was her first ball; pleading, she had begged her father for permission to attend, and he finally, albeit reluctantly, gave in. "Beware, my daughter," he warned, "the snares are strewn like flowers in life." But as soon as her old chaperone turned her back, during a lively waltz, she was struck in the throng by a burning look that reached deep into her soul, making her feel like a bird that suddenly fathomed that it had lived its life in a cage and that there was a big blue sky overhead.

Her mother was an Italian ballerina who converted to Islam to marry the merchant, but a mere three years later, some six months after the birth of her daughter, leapt with a sudden pirouette into the arms of a Spanish bullfighter and ran away with him. The merchant followed the fugitives to Geneva, where, shortly thereafter, a fisherman spotted two shadows flitting about in the water. "There are no trout as big as that!" he reported to the police. Death by accident was the cause written in the death register. The merchant sold his holdings, placed his entire fortune in a Swiss bank account and withdrew in mourning from the worldly doings of Vevey. He had his daughter raised strictly. And though he had always intended to send her back to be brought up properly by a maiden aunt in Cairo, she bore such a striking resemblance to his late wife, whom he still loved despite everything, that he could not bring himself to let her out of his sight. He himself was attached to this accursed place, to which scandal, jealousy and passion kept him shackled, and was ashamed to show his face again among his relatives in Cairo.

How can one describe a beauty such as that of the merchant's daughter? Can alabaster blend with basalt? Are there black pearls or white ebony? She was a green-eyed Nefertiti with a seductive smile, skin as smooth and brown as a chestnut, and hair like black rain.

The Ethiopian was no less pleasing to look upon with his long limbs, his wild black eyes and his finely chiseled mahogany face.

Seeing them strolling together at sunset on the banks of Lake Geneva immediately brought to mind a tale out of *A Thousand and One Arabian Nights*. Like two cats, a wild panther and a sleek Siamese, they stepped quietly along the shore, listened to the whisper of a thousand and one tongues of water and gave no thought to the future or the past—until, finally, one night, alerted by the rattle of an open window, her father became aware of her absence, immediately sent his servants out to find her, and strictly forbade her ever to see the Ethiopian again.

Whereupon the prince sent the merchant countless treasures of ivory, ebony, gold and diamonds, and soon thereafter, dispatched a short note requesting his daughter's hand in marriage.

But the merchant had everything sent back. "The devil take your ivory and your precious stones. It is not because your skin is black," the merchant informed the prince, "that is not the reason I refuse to give you my daughter for a bride, but because I would not have her wed an infidel, a Christian devil—*N'audhubillah!*"

Now the prince secretly begged the merchant's daughter for one last meeting. His wish was transmitted by a bribed servant, and despite her father's ban, difficult as it was to elude his almost sleepless guard—as he had fired the woman who watched over her and stood watch himself— the daughter managed, with the aid of a sedative mixed in with his nightly hookah of tobacco and kif, to slip barefoot out of the house and rush off to her lover.

This time the Ethiopian had a wilder look in his eyes than ever before. She grew frightened at the sight of him, but he took her by the hand and held so tight she could not elude his grip—an unnecessary precaution, since the shackles of love sufficed. Silently he drew her along. She shivered with fear and excitement. Take me where you will, I'll follow! she thought.

For a long, long while, so it seemed to her, they walked without exchanging a single word. Never had the ripple of the lake sounded so loud. A crescent moon hung low in the sky like a Turkish sword. And suddenly he stopped dead in his tracks, turned to her and said: "If not for my eyes, then for none!" And he bit off her nose and spit it out into the water.

Bleeding, she fell in a faint, which is how her father found her the following morning, his fury muffled with fatherly concern.

The merchant had a thousand divers scour the lake bottom in the vicinity of the attack; they finally found the nose, which was successfully reattached, following a long and difficult operation in which the surgeon so skillfully sewed up bone and cartilage and covered it with soft skin taken from her calf, that within three months you had to search with a magnifying glass for the scars pulled back above the cheekbones, leaving an almost unnoticeable flaw that somehow made the whole all the more beautiful, like the glass eyes of the bust of Nefertiti in Berlin.

Protected by diplomatic immunity, the perpetrator escaped.

Not long afterwards, relieved, and nevertheless still cautious, the father gave his daughter as a bride to a well-to-do horse trader from Dubai. Shortly thereafter, pleased at the success of this, his last transaction, the merchant died of a heart attack. But a year later his daughter ran away from the horse trader and traveled to Ethiopia in search of her wild-eyed prince, where they lived happily together and she bore him children as beautiful as the flickering stars on a clear summer night.

Girl on Train

Her hands got to me first, as if they were knitting, not a common scarf, but a cloth to cover the secrets of the heart. The long graceful fingers might just as well have been playing the keys of an arcane instrument, a harpsichord or hurdy-gurdy, now softly, now with a sudden fury, or else engaged in intimate touch—as they looped and dipped with wild abandon on the seat next to mine. Magic wands, not ordinary knitting needles, the sharp points pricked and pierced the twilight and made it bleed in astounding spurts of purple, red and black.

"That's *so* beautiful!" I whispered, seeking an excuse to look up.

"You like it?" She swept back a veil of long black hair, revealing a fine olive complexion and full lips parted with surprise, the startled look of an Italian Madonna just told of the miracle. In a curious kind of harmony with her hands, her black eyes and ruffled brows knitted an ornate tapestry of their own, dazzling and puzzling, purple, red and black.

"Who are you making it for?" I asked with a flirtatious hint, not really wanting to know, picturing the scarf wrapped round my own neck and the fingers entwined with mine.

"For me," she said, "for when it gets cold."

The fingers never stopped knitting and the scarf grew as she spoke, the fringes of its finished end grazing my knee.

"Are you in college?" I asked.

"Oh no," she said, "I'm not smart like that."

"Your color scheme is brilliant!" I insisted.

Whereupon she blushed. "I go to a special school."

—"*Special?*"

—"For slow people."

I choked back a barely audible: "*Oh!*"

The fingers kept dancing and the train rattled on as daylight faded fast and the scarf spilled deep purple all over my lap.

"But I'm learning," she said, "making progress, my teacher tells me. Last week I took a test and you know what? I used to think I was slow, but now,"—like a last splash of sunlight before dusk, a proud smile of radiant beauty lit up her dark eyes and licked the crescent moon of her lips—"now I know I'm average!"

I covered my face with my hands to hide the tears, pretending to muffle a sneeze.

We rolled on in silence, her fingers fondling the dark, the soft woolen shawl of night falling over me.

"This is where I get out," she whispered, drawing back the scarf as the train pulled into the station somewhere in New Jersey, "pleased to have met you, Mister."

Static electricity made my leg hairs stand on end and I trembled, feeling naked. The pleasure was all mine!, I wanted to say, or something to that effect. Too slow to react, I couldn't find the words in time and pressed my eyes shut tight to retrieve the fleeting purple, red and black impression as the train pitched forward into the darkness.

Greetings from Schlemazel Lake

Among the innumerable, lovely and lovely-named lakes in the State of Brandenburg, in Germany, the Schaafsee, Scharmützel, the Witzker, the Wusterwitzer, the two Wannsees, big and little, and the Zermützelsee, there is one you won't find on any map, because it's so minuscule, hardly worth mentioning, actually more of a puffed-up pond, the so-called Schlemazel Lake. There are those who maintain that it does not exist, a bald-faced lie, which I would herewith like to refute. I can confirm its existence from my own personal experience. It sometimes seems to me as if there were a conspiracy against it, as though it were deemed unworthy of watering in the State of Brandenburg.

Where exactly is it located?

How should I know? I was just visiting, on top of which it was so foggy out you couldn't see in front of your nose, really rotten weather, when I accidentally stepped into it, or rather, fell in.

Fortunately, I'm a good swimmer. The strange thing was I didn't get wet, though I swear the water went over my nose. All kinds of fish that I only know smoked, the names of which I am, in any case, not familiar with, swam by me, swiftly and undisturbed. They were not at all surprised to see a lung-breathing creature in their midst.

The local population was also peculiar.

"Where am I?" I asked a man with trout-like features and teensy-weensy eyes I met upon bobbing back up to the surface.

His trout-lips set themselves in slow motion, but not a word came out.

I politely repeated the question. Customs are different everywhere you go.

Whereupon his lips moved more emphatically and he gesticulated with his tail.

That's when I figured he must be deaf and dumb, suspected he had read my lips and expected the same of me.

"I'm terribly sorry," I shook my head, "I can't read lips."

At which point he got all in a huff and beat it.

So I yelled after him: "To hell with you and your schlemazel lake!"

Whereupon the man turned around and blinked back at me with his sad little trout eyes, and it seemed to me that I'd hit the nail on the head.

And when I finally emerged from the pond, though truth to tell, it was not much more than a puddle really, I waggled like a dog to shake off the irrigation. That's when I first noticed that my clothes weren't even wet and was truly amazed at the technical advances made by the textile industry.

And the next day when I sat with my friend Grischa Meyer at a table in the Café Einstein on Unter den Linden, in Berlin, and Grischa asked me where I'd been the day before, I told him about my experience at that peculiar lake.

The waiter came and asked me what I wanted to eat.

"What's on the menu?" I asked.

"Today's special is trout French style."

"How do the French do trout?" I asked, ever hungry for knowledge, particularly of the culinary kind.

But the waiter just turned his back. Which is when I noticed that he was very voluminous, only not up front in the belly, like your typical beery Berliner, but rather in the rear, as if he actually had a tail tucked under his tux.

Strange, I said to myself.

"What's strange?" Asked Grischa.

"The waiter has a tail."

And this discovery spoiled my appetite. So I only ordered a soup with an unpronounceable name, something like Wishywash.

It took a long time for the waiter with the tail to finally bring me my soup, and when I brought a spoonful to my lips I was incensed to discover it was already cold.

"The soup is cold!" I complained.

"Of course it's cold!"

"Wadaya mean, of course!?"

"Wishywash is always cold," the waiter explained.

"The hell with you and your tail and your Wishywash. That's no soup," I screamed. "That's just cold tomato juice in a bowl."

Well the man gave me a piece of his mind in words I can't repeat here.

"Don't be so upset," said Grischa. "It's bad for your heart."

So I got up, said goodbye to Grischa, and went away hungry.

A restaurant you leave hungry, a lake you don't get wet in—strange place, Berlin!

But human memory has a way of bamboozling us, pressed by the oppressive present to mitigate past disappointments. So now when my stomach grumbles but there's nothing that speaks to me on the menu, or when it's so hot in summer that five minutes after I get out of the shower I'm already dripping wet, I think back fondly of Schlemazel Lake.

Let There Be Lies

In the very beginning God procrastinated. Give the deity a break! It was after all his first crack at action! How to formulate the unformed? How to express the unexpressed? How to distinguish between Himself and it all? So many questions! So many headaches! *Oh my God!* He would have exclaimed, had the expression already been invented. But the Lord was expressionless, preliterate, totally self-obsessed and altogether uncreative. God was just a floating glob of ions consumed by colossal sloth, killing eternity. There was no one to blame for his unspecified woes and no one's ear to bend. The Jews, those divine *kvetchers* and scapegoats, hadn't yet come onto the scene; nor had the Catholics with their cozy wood-paneled schmooze booths. He wanted to do something, but not knowing what, was having a Hell of a time of it (another expression that would have come in handy).

"*Aaaarrrrgggggghhhhhhh!*" He moaned in a wordless way, which the sages have since rendered thus (though the gist may have been modified some in the course of multiple translations from Thunder via Ugarit, Hebrew, Greek and Latin Vulgate to contemporary interdenominational

Sermonese): "*Would that there were someone to give voice to my innermost extrovert tendencies! Would that I had a trusted spokesperson, a porte-parole with basic stenographic skills, a winning smile and a cheerful disposition, species and gender unspecified! Thus saith the Lord.*"

But all this wishing was, of course, for naught, a waste of precious eons, since help wanted ads hadn't yet been conceived of, nor was there a rock to engrave or papyrus to so inscribe, or an out of work wordsmith to make it sound good. As frustrated and fed up as He was with the way things were, the Lord did not even have recourse to the ultimate emotional outlet, to take His own name in vain, since no one had heretofore referred to Him, respectfully or in vain, nor had it ever even occurred to Him that such a thing as a name could encapsulate the fluctuating firmament of contradictory and incompatible demiurges raging in His heavenly heart.

"*Aaaaaarrrrrrrgggggggggghhhhhhhhhhh!*" cried the Lord, still louder than before. Which contemporary sages have enucleated thus: "*Thou art so self-centered, it's pathetic!*"

Now the Lord was entranced by the divine echo of His own voice, which, never having heard it before, He mistook for the voice of another. And the Lord looked around, but there was nobody there.

"*Aaaaaaaaaaarrrrrrrrrrrrgggggggggggggggghhhhhhhhhhhh-hhhh!*" He reiterated, this time signifying, according to the sages: "*Go ahead, say it again!*"

"*Aaaaaaaaaarrrrrrrrrrrgggggggggggggghhhhhhhhhhh-hhhh! Go ahead, say it again!*" it said again.

"*Aaaaaaaaaarrrrrrrrrrrgggggggggggggghhhhhhhhhhh-hhhh! Not that, the first thing you said, you fool!*" He said.

"*Aaaaaaaaaarrrrrrrrrrrgggggggggggggghhhhhhhhhhh-hhhh! Not that, the first thing you said, you fool!*" It said back.

(For simplicity's sake, I will cease repeating the Lord's primordial grunts and cut straight to the sages' modern interpolation.)

"*The Hell with you!*" He said, forthwith inventing the expression.

"*The Hell with you!*" it said.

Echoes are dumb and altogether unresponsive, the Lord realized, to his great chagrin. They have a limited recall and can't say anything but the very last thing they heard. God wanted a more engaging confabulator, someone to chew the rag and shoot the breeze with, a sidekick to keep Him company in the dark night of the soul, and so the Lord invented me.

My first press conference—arranged impromptu, haphazardly and altogether unprofessionally, since I had no prior examples to emulate or improve on—good Lord, was that ever a sorry affair, with Himself waiting in the wings, no sound system and no reporters to pose indelicate questions, none yet being in circulation.

"*How did it go?*" He asked me afterwards.

"*Not bad!*" I said, not wanting to jeopardize my job.

"*Good*," said God, "*let's do it again sometime.*"

Fortunately for both of us, He immediately forgot all about it and never even brought it up again till the interview at Sinai, by which time He had mastered his communication skills and no longer needed my assistance. But back then, God had other fish to fry. First things first, God felt the fire in his loins and wanted to find himself a special someone for intimate starlight dinners.

"*God*," I tried to put it to Him gently, "*in case Thou hast not noticed, there are no available unattached divas around, Thou being a monotheistic all-encompassing concept.*"

"*Nonsense*," He fumed, "*I'll create one!*"

Now I will tell you how the infinitely resourceful Lord God, Our Father, King of the Universe (and of all as of yet undiscovered space) found and fashioned himself a date out of water vapor, there being no personals column to appeal or respond to, no singles club events to attend or websites to peruse. God glanced around, and nearsighted as He was, never having focused His divine gaze on anything farther removed than His left toe, He spotted a billowy cloud, a flighty puffy nubile nimbus, and promptly fell for it.

"*Let me shape it to my liking!*" said the Lord. So God got to work and gave that cloud a divine makeover, squeezing and kneading until he truly liked the result. Alright, so she was no great shakes by modern standards, no centerfold material, hardly a Helen of Troy. His beloved puff piece would not exactly turn heads on today's street corners, but look at the tush on the tiny Venus of Willendorf, that Cro-Magnon fetish, for heaven's sake! He was wanting. She was willing.

"*Listen up, spokesperson!*" He commanded me (my first full-fledged assignment). "*I want you to compose a love letter to my precious little cloud, tell her just how much she means to me, warm her up for a little thunderstorm, so to speak.*"

"*I'll do my best, Lord!*" I said, and skywrit forthwith the following epistle in cirro-maculate script:

My Dearest Powder Puff,

Thou makest me want to set a sun in the heavens for thee to block, harness a gentle wind to carry thee about on its back, and shape a globe for thee to shadow!

Affectionately thine,

God

P.S. Baby, I just love the way thou waftest.

"*Good*," said God. "*Go ahead and do it!*"

"*Hold it, Lord!*" I said. "I'm only Thy humble spokesperson, remember! Thou makest me take dictation, edit a little here and there, add a little flourish. Don't get me wrong, my cup runneth over with gratitude. But Thou hast not endowed me with divine creative ability!"

"*Thou art more lowly than an echo!*" He shouted, enraged. "*Get thee out of my sight, pipsqueak! Behold! Watch what God can do when He sets His mind to it!*"

Verily I did tremble as I looked. For then and there the

Lord God, King of the Universe, etc. blinked, fashioning a great ball of fire with the gleam of His naked eye and hurled it into the heavens. The effort involved made Him break wind in four different directions, loosening His celestial sphincter, pores and all other orifices. And the Lord sweated dew and peed rain. And then—I don't know quite how to put it—He expelled from his posterior a globular mass that would become the world. I duly noted down the names of everything, Sun, Wind, Rain, Earth, according to the sounds He made. All this to impress the cloud.

But the cloud, being the flighty nebulous thing that it was, let itself be carried away by one of the very winds its divine admirer fashioned to carry it around on its back.

"*God damn it!*" cried the Lord, then and there creating blasphemy. And in his jealous rage He hurled a barrage of high voltage bolts of lightning, reducing his erstwhile paramour to a cirrocumulus cluster. And before I could stop Him, He went on a rampage, whacking and kicking, smashing and crashing, cracking and completely messing up his initially perfect love-inspired universe. Now all was off kilter, out of whack. The sun split open, subdividing into the moon and the stars. The wind whipped itself up into a cosmic storm of comets that wreaked havoc clear across creation. The rain leaked out of the shattered vessel the Lord had created to hold it and drowned the world, itself now a lopsided lumpy thing that has been spinning at a tilt ever since.

"*For God's sake,*" I said (inventing the expression), "*look what Thou hast done, Lord. Thou hast made a mess of Thy creation!*"

"*It's all thy fault, spokesperson!*" He said, like all big shots, passing the buck. "*Why did thou not stop me!*"

"*Go ahead, blame me, Lord, if it makes Thee feel any better,*" I shrugged, "*but it's a lie and thou knowest it!*"

So now I'm out of a job. What do I do next? Tell-all celebrity biographies are big. Think maybe I'll take a stab, cash in on my inside knowledge. What have I got to lose? *Bubble… Babble…Idle…Libel…* I haven't yet decided on a title.

II

True Confessions

The Disease of Self

What the doctor can't cure is a point of pride, a condition inscribed in DNA and nonsense. There are over-the-counter remedies you could take but they just hold off the inevitable. If only you were a worm, which, when cut in two, could grow a new head and tail, or didn't even bother, but just kept wiggling along, taking things in stride. At the border between night and day even the shadows evaporate. Dreams scatter like vampires afraid of the light. The sleepless are compelled to embrace the disease of self.

Midmoon

The early hours belong neither to yesterday nor to tomorrow. As there is midday and midnight, so should there also be a stretch of time—call it midmoon— between the indigo breakdown and the powdery blue busyness of dawn, the timeless refuge of insomniacs.

* * *

My neck is creaking. The nail on my right thumb, the one holding down the pen, has split open, staining the pen shaft red.

* * *

Oh, sleep, what have I ever done to displease you? True, I stole a couple of dreams and pawned them off as poems, but where's the harm in that? I just wanted to broadcast your brilliance, to needle the night. Forgive me, sleep, my precious!

* * *

I flee the living room and seek refuge in the kitchen. Why are kitchen tabletops always sticky? Ledgers of domesticity, they reveal more about the viscous love of family than all the fabricated grins in photo albums. The tick of the kitchen clock drives me mad. It's time getting to me, that fiction I always denied, that wilting thing that bleaches hair and illusions. Time is a tyrant. Time is a trap. If only it flew, as the saying goes. But it strangles. As if each little parcel of our passing were really equal in duration and intensity. As if eternity were divisible and we could measure its shrinking in dead seconds frozen in flight. Why does the refrigerator sing at night?

* * *

In a sleepless state not far removed from madness all is metaphor, like the loose screws on the frame of my glasses and the cracks in the ceiling. The unidentified street sounds strike like auditory shrapnel hurled by a roving militia. The boxed destinies of cars and trucks deliver somebody else's tomorrow.

* * *

No choice in the eternal tick-tock that stretches, sleepless, till dawn, no choice, after the rage of helplessness breaks, but to sit back and watch, like on a long train ride, when life is a landscape rushing by, a succession of trees, homes, shrubs, depots, ducks and cows—and people scattered about, mostly in clusters, but sometimes solitary. No choice but to watch and love it for what it is, the ringside seat at a non-stop hundred-ring circus, the wildest beast being me in the cage of my skull put through the motions by the great lion tamer. Nothing to do but admire it all, the décor framed by the window, the concert of waking birds, the percussion of the trucks—an endless opera.

* * *

The first yawn breaks like an avalanche. It clouds your glasses, drawing tears, as if the eyes were sponges that drain when they've seen too much.

* * *

In the symphony of the waking family, the toilets play percussion, the radio alarm hits a high note, stomachs grumble arpeggios to the piccolo of hungry sparrows. I am the reluctant conductor by default, because I don't play an instrument. The creaking floorboards and opened doors applaud.

A Warning Concerning Autocannibalism

Do not eat yourself, others, if you must, but refrain from your own flesh, however tempting, or there'll be nothing left when you need it. From time to time you may bite a lip or suck on a hair. There is documented evidence of one desperate case, a ship's captain marooned on a desert island, who fed first on his right leg and then on his left, and by the time he was rescued was down to the thumb, index and middle finger of his right hand, fist clenched, bravely resisting temptation. I don't know what I would have done, he is reported to have said, if they hadn't found me when they did. The repressed autocannibal feeds on his own thoughts, turning them over and over, savoring the scent. Some spend their entire lives salivating over a single notion. Others, more rabid, need a new idea every second to break open and suck out the marrow. There are repressed autocannibals in high places, government, industry and the military, who secretly long to devour themselves. Only discipline (the science of self-denial) and the desire to devour others, the enemy, the competition, friends, keeps them in line, though they do have trouble deciding who's edible.

Mother Tongue...Father Mouth, a Lullaby

The couple attempts a heart-to-heart talk, only no words come out.

Open up, the woman motions the man in sign language, let's have a look, see what's wrong. Teeth, tongue, larynx, everything appears to be in order.

"Let *me* have a look!" the daughter, not quite two, suddenly bursts into speech, mimicking her mother's concern.

The parents' jaws drop, knees buckle under, now they are really speechless.

"Why the big surprise?" the daughter asks, grabbing and playing with her father's and mother's tongues, tugging at them, trying to tear them out. "Sing me a song, a duet!" she demands.

Prostrated before their daughter, both held fast by their tongue, as if on a leash, the parents grunt a well-known lullaby, the one about the baby in the treetop, but without words.

Though the tune is off and the sound hardly soothing, both succumb to the soporific effect and fall fast asleep.

In the man's dream, the woman is the first to awaken; in the woman's dream it's the opposite—that's pretty much the only difference—except that in the man's dream, the daughter turns into his dead mother and keeps tugging at his tongue, as if she were tolling a church bell, whereas daughter and mother merely switch places in the woman's dream, each tugging at the man's tongue, but more like a doorbell.

"Who's that?" asks the daughter (formerly his dead mother)—in the man's dream—pointing at him. "He looks very familiar."

"It's only the deaf and dumb man in the dream," his dead mother (formerly his daughter—the roles, it turns out, are reversible) replies with a matter-of-fact shrug.

In the woman's dream, the child swallows the man whole like a python a pig.

"You must learn to share," the woman protests in her sleep.

Meanwhile, wide awake, the little girl giggles.

The Secret Life of Brush and Shoe, According to Barbie

S he claims the leather upper craves the rub of bristles. What of it! That the hairbrush lives for the lick of the shoe's moist tongue. So what! It's just the gossip of a Barbie doll* that doesn't understand what she sees but likes to watch the brush work up a sweat. The scraping thrills her plastic loins. The futility of such an idle rub under the glass-topped coffee table, the fact that they can never have babies merely makes their love all the safer and sadder. Still, she cannot help but wonder what the child would look like, the color of its eyes, the tufts of bristle sprouting from its sole. At least it would learn to walk early. Painfully aware of her own limitations, the doll takes pleasure in imagined romance just as my daughter does with her, making her do un-childlike things.

---

* "When I conceived Barbie, I believed it was important to a little girl's self-esteem to play with a doll that has breasts." Ruth Handler (creator of Barbie and co-founder of Mattel, Inc.), Dream Doll, The Ruth Handler Story, by Ruth Handler with Jacqueline Shannon, Stamford, Conn., 1995.

Fathers and Sons

1

MY TURTLE SON

It happened during wartime. My son was born a turtle. How does a turtle take caresses? I fretted. How would I cuddle and care for him? But then I fathomed the utility of his condition, a tactical advance for mankind, a doubling back to our amphibious roots. That he would be safer that way, able to withdraw into his shell at the hint of danger. He shat like any other child. Like any other parent I had to clean him up. And like any parent, I loved him because he was mine. Flesh of my flesh, blood of my blood. I did worry sometimes. How would he be perceived by others? How would he adjust? But my turtle son did not seem the least bit concerned about his state. In any case, he knew no other and might well wonder, when consciousness comes, why his father lacked a shell, and how in heaven's name I would survive without protection in wartime. They were after us again, and a shell would doubtless have come in handy.

2

FENCING WITH MY INFANT SON

Fencing, as usual, with my infant son D'Artagnan at dinner last night, I accidentally speared him in the neck with a steak knife. Pick up your fork and parry! Go ahead, defend yourself! I pleaded. Pierce my vitals, show me your love! I cried, concerned, lest I forfeit my finest opponent yet. The spectators, our dinner guests, were evenly divided, some clamoring for seconds, some patiently awaiting the dessert.

3

WHY THE SON TAKES A WIFE

A son is peeling pieces off his mother. I am not a banana or some sweet tropical fruit, she bitterly complains. Oblivious to her protests, accustomed as he is to sucking her for sustenance, the son rips off his daily portion. Mothers are high in cholesterol and rich in calories, she tries to scare him off. I am young, says the son, I don't care what I eat. Soon, if you don't watch it, she warns, there won't be anything left of me. Never mind, he says, then I'll just have to find a wife.

Essential Smell

Of late I have begun to smell like boiled potatoes left too long in the pot.

In childhood I went through my sea scallop, lamb chop, spiced ham, and sour pickle periods.

In adolescence my private scent, a rarefied peanut butter and jelly musk, spiked with essence of anchovy paste, to which only my solipsist nostrils were attuned, lodged in the pit of my left wrist—the left arm being the boney conduit to the central dynamo of self. I did not like being touched by others, as it spoiled my essential smell.

But as I grew older, and less risk-averse, that private essence dispersed, mingling with and sometimes even overpowered by the essence of others, exiled to the far corners of sensory consciousness, sometimes seeping from the armpits and between the legs, sometimes clinging to the hairs of my burgeoning mustache, threatening to jump ship.

Some gave off the scent of hot chestnuts, sizzling pizza cheese, others emanated ozone after the rain.

One old flame smelled like roast chicken. Unless I

focused on something else, my nostrils quivered in her presence, aroused by the savor of an oven stuffer pouring out of her every pore. It was admittedly a bit incestuous, my mother's family having been in the poultry business, but that was part of the thrill. Every time things got steamy between us it felt like swimming in chicken soup. Overpowering at first, the aroma made me want to devour her, chomp on the breast, gnaw at the legs, naturally saving the tail for last. But the fickle olfactory appeal eventually wore off, or rather inverted from attraction to revulsion: like getting intimate with Frank Purdue.

I fell in love with my wife because she smelled like warm French bread fresh out of the oven, and because her smell melded so well with mine, sandwiching me in, so to speak, in the soft dough of her embrace. It was my cold cuts period, Hungarian salami in a sweat, Prosciutto di Parma after a shower.

Our scents traveled, hers dripping from her earlobes and gathering in the delicate dip of her shoulder blades, mine descending from wrists to fingertips and knuckles, and settling in the fine hairs sprouting from the index fingers on either hand.

Over the years both of our essential smells fermented the way fine spirits do, hers into that of a single malt Scotch whiskey from the Isle of Islay, and mine, considerably less refined, into that of a homemade Polish potato vodka.

It was during my last conversation with my mother that the matter, in a manner of speaking, came to a boil.

"What are you thinking?" I asked.

"When the potatoes are soft," the great mother hen intoned with a certain oracular intensity, "you have to peel them." Whereupon her head fell sideways on the pillow and lay still.

Last words have a way of lingering, like smells.

Long after my mother's passing, I lay beside my wife, distracted, pondering my mother's last words, wondering if she had meant them literally or metaphorically. Had she been hallucinating a pot boiling on the stove, enunciating a recipe for happiness, or sending me a last message to buck up and do what I had to do while there was still time?

"Honey," I whispered to my wife, inhaling her intoxicating peaty essence. But my own fermented potato vodka odor intruded on any attempt at intimacy. "I won't be a minute," I said, "I need to shower."

I washed and washed but could not wash away the smell of old potatoes. My skin started peeling, as it had in childhood after a bad sunburn, when, perversely, I had helped it along, peeling off dried-up flaps.

I stripped off the flap of epidermis dangling around the fingernail of my left pinky tip, baring the pink surface of the flesh underneath. In the jet of hot water it stung where I peeled it.

"Come to bed!" my wife called with distilled intensity.

"I'm not done washing yet!" I called back, sucking and sniffing at the wound, enticed by my newfound essence of steak tartar.

Warning: Reader (In) Discretion Advised

"Oh you're in shape alright, but it ain't good shape!"
Anonymous remark

So you think you're safely invisible, do you!? Think we can't look into your living room right this very moment?!

Think again!

The scene is all too predictable. The two of you sit watching T.V., a rerun of *The Honeymooners*, or *All in the Family*, or some other idyll of life, munching on potato chips. In fact, your better half's not watching the show. She's reading a book—*this* book, why not!?

You're laughing, not because you find the situation comedy on screen particularly funny (you've already seen this episode at least a dozen times before and know exactly what they're going to say and do next), but following the lead of the invisible laughers, you, too, feel obliged to titter.

"What happened, dear?" she asks, looking up from the book in her lap, wanting to share a common experience (to combat the growing sense of domestic alienation documented in a recent issue of *TIME*, in which it is purported that more than 50% of American couples won't stick it out).

You just shrug, because it wasn't that funny really, and you're ashamed to admit it.

Comes a pause in the program, an advertisement for cars, and then another for Ronzoni spaghetti, one of New York's natural resources, along with Swingline Staples.

"Hon?" you hesitate, testing the waters with a smile (because you, too, have read the same survey in *TIME*).

"What is it, sweetheart?"

But now the T.V. is advertising physical fitness, and the two of you are definitely not, by T.V. standards, physically fit.

Another car commercial.—"Christ, you'd think the City must surely have bought enough cars by now to fill every square inch of blacktop from East Side to West, bumper to bumper!" your significant other remarks, having caught the tail end of the ad.

You nod with a smug grin, touching your middle, wondering if she's noticed that you've had to let out your belt another notch and how far removed you are from the masculine ideal lauded a moment ago.

Now the ideal T.V. couple is traveling to Bermuda, after buying new clothes for the trip with their American Express card, smiling all the while.

That dress wouldn't fit me, she worries surreptitiously

with envy and disgust, catching a glimpse of her ideal counterpart's firm rounded hips.

Another commercial. Another pitch for physical fitness. As if it weren't enough to sit quietly at home for an evening! As if middle age were a crime, for Christ's sake!

Meanwhile, your wife is thinking: I wonder if he likes the T.V. broad better than me. Her teeth are perfectly straight and her toosh is tight, she seethes, particularly self-conscious about her thighs, which have begun to wobble, Jell-O-like, when she walks.

Another car commercial. It's enough to give you carbon monoxide poisoning. Now a beer commercial, which makes you thirsty as it's supposed to.

She senses your thirst, gets up, goes to the kitchen and gets you a beer. What an angel!

"Thanks, hon!"

Now the governor of New Jersey is complaining about pollution and waste. He's got some nerve! They practically invented the problem! And a garbage bag manufacturer up next takes advantage of the governor's righteous indignation to advertise the durability of its product.

Already you're feeling a little guilty for the empty beer can and the bits of potato chip crumbs you carelessly let fall and kicked under your easy chair, knowing she'll clean up the mess later.

One show leads to another. Nothing really funny. It's

awful, you think, how T.V. underestimates your I.Q.!

"Honey!?" you caress her wobbly thigh. You're no spring chicken yourself, and it's been a long time since you felt like it.

"What is it, Sweetheart?"

Then the telephone rings.

You let it ring, not wanting to interrupt the moment.

But she reaches for the receiver.—"For you, dear!"

It's your proctologist's secretary, the one you've secretly had the hots for, calling to ask if you'd mind the presence of T.V. cameras at your next appointment. NBC news is doing a segment on the risks of rectal cancer, and would you, she wonders, in so many words, mind baring your bottom for public edification. You hesitate a moment, pondering your one likely shot at 15 minutes of fame, but finally decline, figuring if any part of you had to become famous you'd rather it be your face.

"What did they want?" your wife wants to know.

"Nothin'." you mutter, embarrassed, because the invisible laughers are back responding on cue and it feels like they're laughing at you.

I'm Not Myself

My feet, stomach and forehead are inherited from my father, my dark curly hair from my mother, my voice from my maternal grandfather. My walk is his too, I'm told. Only my worries are my own.

This morning, a woman I've never met, a perfect stranger, walks up to me as I am about to descend the steps at my regular subway station on my way to work and whips out the wallet-size snapshot of a child.—"That's her!" she half-howls half-hisses with a strangely insinuating sneer.

I don't know what to say, feeling the eyes of the morning rush of passers-by upon me, and fearing that I am about to be wrongfully and publicly accused of paternity, kidnapping, rape or worse.

The woman keeps staring. "Don't you recognize her?!" she insists with considerable emotion. "You finally delivered her after five miscarriages. You *are* Dr....!"

"I'm afraid you're mistaken, ma'am!" I shake my head with a half-hearted shrug, all choked up for reasons I cannot rightly explain, then and there doubting my own identity, her tone of assurance overpowering my own wavering doubt.

Her piercing gaze cuts me like a scalpel. "But you look so much like him!" She keeps staring, clearly hoping to break down my stubborn resistance and make me recant, even as I race down the subway steps, shaken to the core. And though I adamantly maintain that the woman and the child in the picture are complete strangers, there is little doubt that had I been hauled off for interrogation, I would have failed a lie detector test.

But that is only the beginning.

Arriving at work, I find a curt message left on my answering machine by a collection agency located in Arizona, on behalf of their client company in Virginia, assuring me that, if I act immediately I will not face prosecution, but reminding me of my outstanding debt.

What debt?

A call to the collection agency reveals that I, or someone pretending to be me, has apparently purchased a cell phone and proceeded to ring up a telephone bill of $10,000 at last count.

"But I don't even know how to use a cell phone!" I protest, which, in this day and age, the collection agency agent in Arizona finds hard to believe. My options, she says, are to pay up immediately or file a police report and attempt to clear my record with three credit bureaus located in Georgia, California and Texas, who never answer their phone.

Whereupon I hasten to the local precinct.

"You may or may not," says the detective on duty, eying me suspiciously, "be the victim of identity theft."

—"What's that?"

—"Someone out there pretending to be you!"

—"How is that possible?"

"The imposter," he says, "might have apprehended your name and digital data (social security number, date of birth etc.) from a garbage bag, a hospital record or a conversation fragment overheard in passing—especially from a cell phone."

—"But I don't own a cell phone!"

"My advice to you," he says, "is to exercise extreme caution in all future interactions, shred your garbage, filter your calls."

My upset exceeds the strictly financial.

I have stopped answering the phone and suspect every stranger in the crowd.

It's an outmoded metaphysical dilemma, very 19th-century, very Poe-like, I admit. Contemporary consumer society has no modern recourse or remedy for the Doppelgänger syndrome.

If the culprit was shrewd enough to tap into my vital codes, could he not just as easily break into the private precincts of my life? Mimic my manner? Sign my name to restaurant checks, contracts, love letters and bylines? Charm my children? Woo my wife?

And may he not at this very minute be dwelling on me as I am on him, reading this very text as a way to read my mind, predict my next move and beat me to it? Chances are he's a smoother, and I suspect, far more polished version of me than myself.

My bank, until recently a low-key neighborhood operation geared to financial simpletons such as myself, was taken over by a foreign-based international conglomerate with an intimidating acronym. When I stop by at lunchtime to deposit a check and verify the status of my accounts, the teller almost pushes me to tears. All the account numbers and modes of transaction, which it has taken me years to memorize and master, have been altered. I am obliged to fill out three complete sets of withdrawal and deposit slips before getting it right, all the while enduring a barely suppressed snicker from behind the bullet-proof window and the smoldering protest of the growing line of customers behind.

"Tell me," I ask the teller, "has anyone else tried to access my money?"

"No one," he sneers, "other than you!"

And when I get home, the children glance up from their perch at the TV set as if I were a total stranger, clearly more in tune with the people on screen.

"It's me!" I cry.

My wife flashes me a quizzical look. "You're not yourself today, honey!" she says, confirming my worst suspicions.

III

True Encounters

Gertrude and Alice Pose

That, my dear Alice, is a device employed by the lazy voyeur to entrap his prey, Gertrude warns loud enough to be overheard by the man behind the camera. It reminds me of a Cyclops, Alice shudders. Precisely, Alice dear, says Gertrude gripping the arms of her easy chair, which is why we'd best be inconspicuous.—Will you have a cup of tea, Mr. Man Ray? The photographer declines. Gertrude concentrates hard, determined to become the chair. How dearly the walls love Alice, who easily melds with mildew and art. Gertrude is jealous at such natural facility, but too proud to show it. Sit up straight, she admonishes her companion, posterity has no patience for bad posture.

Where is Singer?

The old man seated beside me awaiting the appearance of the celebrated author Isaac Bashevis Singer at The Workman's Circle Auditorium is becoming a pest. From a rumpled brown shopping bag he pulls out and shamelessly shows off photographs of his grandchildren, to which I offer the obligatory compliments. Light and sound technicians, meanwhile, test the mike and spot, inadvertently knocking the beam off-kilter. The veins in the old man's ears catch the light like insects trapped in amber. Squinting, he scans the room with a laser-like intensity—a retired diamond cutter from 47th Street, no doubt.

Everybody wants to be in the spotlight nowadays.

If only he'd shut up and let me flirt with the bookishly bespectacled beauty to my left.

Little by little, the hall fills up. Coughs and whispers proliferate. Legs are crossed and uncrossed. I crane my neck, scanning the crowd. "So where is Singer?" I wonder aloud, glancing repeatedly at my watch.

"That *ganef* is always late!" the old man shakes his head with a tisk of disapproval and a rakish wink at the girl, fingering the books in his bag, purchased second-hand for signing, I assume.

The M.C. steps up to the mike. "It is my very great honor...etc."

But where is Singer?

"Excuse me," the old man rises with a mischievous grin, having managed in the meantime to get the girl's number. "I think I'm wanted on stage!"

Have I Heard of You?

The following encounter with the late William Packard, poet, playwright, teacher, and publisher of the literary journal *The New York Quarterly*, and a postal worker took place at the Chelsea Station Post Office in New York. I immediately recognized the man in front of me on the package pickup line as my old teacher, his tousled hair, coat pockets stuffed with manuscripts, and an unlit cigarette dying to be smoked dangling from his lips, a dead give-away.

"I took your playwriting class some years back," I said.

"Oh yeah? Are you still writing?"

"Yes."

"What are you reading?"

"Kleist."

"Too morbid for me," the postal worker piped in, "I don't like German writers."

"Oh yeah?" Packard bristled.

"Don't like Americans much either," he added.

"You're talking to two authors of the English language," William Packard solemnly declared.

"English I like," said the postal worker, "Anthony Powell, now there's a novelist."

Packard's package picked up, he stormed off. The postal worker turned to me.

"A poet, huh?"

I nodded.

"Poets," he opined, "they all think they're Walt Whitmans nowadays. What about you?" he asked, studying my name on the official yellow post office pickup slip. "Have I heard of you?"

Dolly, the Pancake Queen

There are virtuosos in every endeavor. So why not fast food? To have seen her in action in her heyday was to witness a colossal force of nature, like Maui or Mount Saint Helena or the legendary Vesuvius blowing its stack, the destructive potential curtailed and channeled by stainless steel and Formica.

At lightning speed, Dolly, the queen of Mondo's, an all-night dive in Boston's Haymarket Square back in the Seventies before its gentrification, ladled out the milky white lava in neat ringlets onto the sizzling griddle with one hand, while with the other cracking egg after egg and dropping the glistening goo in even yellow and white islands in the sea of grease, beside shriveled strips of bacon, mountains of hash browns and a massive cauldron of steaming black coffee.

Dolly's head kept rocking all the while, her massive bosom heaving, arms flying, eyes bulging like the yolks. Her devotion to the task was total and unquestioning, more a matter of instinct than training, for she was a Picasso of the skillet, a Zen yogi of yolks, never over- or undercooking an egg, piercing its yellow eye, or marring the contour and circumference of a pancake.

Her one indulgence, if you could call it that, was the cigarette forever dangling (contrary to Department of Health regulations) from her puckered lips.

Tipped off, the Department of Health once sent an undercover inspector who issued a citation noting the ash in the vortex of his sunny-side-up.

Dolly was suspended, but her loyal all night clientèle of truckers, hookers, cabbies and miscellaneous loners complained of the languor of her skinny replacement, and lest the graveyard shift take their business to the competition, White Castle, Dunkin' Donuts, or, heaven forbid, McDonald's, the new kid on the block, Dolly was soon back on the job, a live volcano, smoke spewing from her spout, calling out teakettlelike: *"WHAT'LL IT BE!?"*

New York Nude

"The city is human nature posing nude," wrote Lincoln Steffens, late 19th-century police reporter for the *New York Post*. For a fleeting moment before the fall New York continued to oblige.

I

More London limey green, pea-soup-stained than Manhattan-chowder-red, the fog descended one warm summer night, spilling unctuously over sidewalk and street, blurring the borders between person and thing. It smothered all but the headlights of oncoming cars, turned strident red traffic lights into timid pink reminders of danger ahead, and slowed the ordinarily frenetic pace of life to a dream-like crawl. Prudent pedestrians extended wary fingers and stiff toes, like the canes of the blind, shuffling cautiously so as not to collide, trip on cracks or tumble off the curb.

And so it came as something of a surprise, even to the jaded Downtown contingent, when, carelessly strolling up MacDougal Street, out of the green-gray haze, an indecipherable ectoplasm advanced, bulbous and bubblegum-colored, suddenly sprouting arms, limbs and a head. A naked man, oblivious to the startled looks of passersby, he was dressed in nothing but a smile. But by the same ineluctable twist that produced this irregular weather condition, public response to such an unheard-of fashion statement elevated rapidly from hushed amazement to light-hearted amusement, interspersed with titters of laughter, pivoting from tolerant shrugs to scandalized anger on the one hand, and grudging admiration and outright envy on the other—if only *I* dared follow his lead!

Too late, the anger, envy and longing lingered a while only to be shrugged off as childish shame –by which time, in any case, the emperor's new clothes had long since been cloaked by the fog.

2

While all around it, old warehouses, depots and loading docks are undergoing expensive facelifts, to be born again as high-end restaurants, cafés and fashion boutiques, a stubborn hold-out, the Baby Doll Lounge, surely merits landmark status. Its blackened plywood shutters and weathered marquee defy gentrification. Inside, divided down the middle with a curtain strung like a loin cloth, as per city ordinance, the dancers perform fully clothed in the antechamber and stripped down to a g-string in the back room.

Needless to say, most clients gravitate to the rear, where two spry dancers, one svelte black, one wiry white, glistening with sweat like polished ebony and ivory, take turns curling their legs round a greased metal pole probably salvaged from an old fire house. Passé perhaps, but oh so voluptuous, each plays her instrument solo, writhing, quivering, vibrato, stroking herself like a rare Stradivarius, not a note off key, muscles twitching in unexpected parts, working herself up to a crescendo that brings the house down.

Landmarks Commission, better come quickly!

Dancing Fool

Slipping, sliding, rhythmically writhing on a scrap of linoleum unfurled beneath Times Square, just beyond the platform where the "S" Shuttle secretes its load of humanity, a bone-thin man with jet black, slicked-back hair whisks his willowy partner through a Latin dance routine. Tipping and turning her tightly sheathed torso, he thrusts a knee lasciviously between her pliant limbs for a torrid tango, the two of them practically going at it right then and there, when it suddenly dawns on the spectator in an unsettling flash, that the dancer's partner is a doll, a skillfully stuffed appendage born of old socks and stifled libido.

Unabashed, the artificial duo strut their stuff for the catcalling crowd. Several questions beg asking.

How long have they been an item and an act?

Were there earlier incarnations? (Fred Astaire famously tripped the light fantastic on screen with a compliant mop, Gene Kelley waltzed a wet umbrella.)

How, where, when was such an astonishing spectacle first conceived and received?

Were he/they applauded, taunted, jeered, assaulted in

some smoky back room in Buenos Aires?

Did a scandalized undercover man of the cloth stride forward and tear the tenuous twosome apart?

Did the dancer secretly welcome the attack, not as a violation, but, rather, as a violent affirmation of his art?

Here is my theory.

Seeing his sister-self in shreds, he cried and cursed him/them-self/selves at having gone public. But later, years later, in a single-room-occupancy hotel in Spanish Harlem, his partner was reborn, more radiant than ever, red-cheeked, drenched in cheap perfume, a plastic rose planted in her tightly braided hair, henceforth to tour the underground platforms of this world with him—in flagrant duality—and one day, perhaps, if the mood is right, to conceive a dancing heir!

Beat It!

On the middle level of the ever moving station stop at Roosevelt Avenue, Jackson Heights, Queens, where the subway and the elevated meet in a shaky embrace and humanity flows on a non-stop escalator between heaven and earth, the melting pot boils over with new arrivals as trains disgorge their load. Here reed-flute players from the Andes, Mariachi orchestras from Mexico, Chinese erhu players, Flamenco guitarists, ventriloquists, acrobats and virtuosos of every description perform their exotic acts.

On a recent Sunday the crowd pressed to the right of the stairs in a long drawn-out amorphous ring, from the midst of which emanated deafening music. Even the two Jehovah's Witnesses stationed stiff as wax figures to the left of the stairs gave up God's business for the moment and joined the onlookers, since nobody seemed to be interested in their message.

The object of everyone's rapt attention remained a mystery to the chance passerby until suddenly the wall of humanity parted a crack, revealing a tiny figure mistakable at first sight for a little boy, but soon recognizable—on account of the powerful shoulders—as an adult dwarf.

With a black hat set at a dapper tilt, dark sunglasses and a tight black sequined jacket, he moved gracefully and rhythmically backwards, in the soft stepping, faked forward motion of Michael Jackson's trademark moonwalk, transforming the filthy, chewing-gum-flecked, floor into his stage.

Blasting from a somewhat battered boom-box, the familiar androgynous voice of the pop star bid the crowd to beat it as the dwarf abruptly grabbed his private parts, and with shoulders flung back, obscenely heaving his hips, dry-humped the air before him. Some snickered, others cheered at the shrill command. Whereupon, after lowering the jacket slowly, provocatively, first from the left shoulder, then from the right, to demonstrate with rippling muscles the amazing strength of his arms, he started trembling suggestively, ever more unabashedly, first with the chest cage, next with the stomach muscles, and finally with his entire body, consumed by a carefully choreographed orgasm. Some spectators laughed out loud. Others turned red, covering their children's eyes.

But they did the dancer an injustice. For his dance was at once a great tribute and an extraordinary send-up, in which he invested his entire being and a remarkable comic talent altogether worthy of Aristophanes and Harpo Marx.

The crowd fell silent as the song came to an end, and the dwarf took a slow bow, his hat pushed back, his glasses pressed down over his nose, his sadly noble, strikingly handsome Latin Mestizo face held up like a hidden treasure with the pride of a true artist and the desperation of an eternal outsider. For a split second his size was forgotten. In that instant he also revealed a striking resemblance to the fallen pop star. Coins and crumpled banknotes flew through the air. Every injured soul saw himself reflected in that face. And as the spectators scattered, the two Jehovah's Witnesses surreptitiously slinking back into their corner, the dwarf deftly swept up his take, whereupon with hat, glasses and expression once again set aright, he bit his lower lip and prepared to be born again in the next dance.

Beyond the Borders of
Marlboro Country

B illed as a living wonder—alongside Michael the
Illustrated Man, every square inch of whose
epidermis is a tattooed tapestry; Santina the Rubber
Girl, a sultry contortionist girded in a fur bikini, who
can wave goodbye and wink bent over between her
legs; a two-headed calf, and a seven-legged pig, among
other anomalies of nature—Otis, The Human Cigarette
Machine, a laconic black man born without arms or
legs, performs every half hour on the hour in a dank
dark boardwalk arcade at the corner of 12th and Surf in
Coney Island, Brooklyn.

Extending an agile tongue, he plucks a sheath from an
open pack of rolling papers, scoops up and deposits a tight
line of tobacco, wraps the paper round the weed, shaping
and fitting it with the precision of a master tailor, and licks
it shut. Then, resting the white tube on the back of a box of
wooden kitchen matches, he tongue-butts the matchbox
open, plucks out a match stick from the other side, tips
up the cigarette, and without missing a beat, strikes the
match-head against the strip of flint, lights up and inhales

like his life depended on it, as indeed it does.

For his grand finale, Otis flips the cigarette over on his tongue, burning tip inwards, takes a toke, exhaling fire, dragon-like, from his fluttering nostrils, sucks in the butt and gulps, smacking his lips, only now breaking the silence. "I think I put it out," he coyly grins, "but if I didn't, somebody please bring me a glass of water!"

The glass is fetched by Santina on cue, whom Otis salutes, cobra-like, with an obscene vibrato of the tongue, before tipping it up and downing its contents. Biting hard on the rim with tobacco-stained teeth and a winsome smile, he proffers the plastic chalice for tips.

"No pictures, please," he quips, "I'm wanted in four states by 12 angry wives!"—peddling black and white collectible postcards of himself, a dollar apiece.

After the Storm

In the immediate wake of the storm nothing worked. Neither power nor light, neither running water nor heat, neither internet nor ATM machine, the fundamentals of middle class life without which we don't believe we can live happily nowadays. On the fifth day, as if following an abbreviated biblical prototype, the flood receded, creation started up again, and there was light, if only uptown, and the subway was running again, but only up to 34th Street.

Downtown remained in the dark. I made myself somewhat presentable and shared a cab to Penn Station with two well-dressed gents in suit and tie, a Caucasian and a Chinese (a white and a yellow man, as we say in popular parlance), who, like me, commuted to work. All three of us complained about the inconveniences of the last week and wished each other a pleasant day, i.e. a speedy return to normalcy.

Then I climbed out of the taxi and transferred to an uptown A-Train. The subway was free of charge for a change. A small compensation. Gift of the MTA. The train, otherwise stuffed like a sausage with human flesh, a conveyance that ordinarily waited for nothing and no one, lingered, laid back, in the station, as if with all the time in the world. I had ample occasion to study my fellow passengers. Directly opposite me sat a somewhat plump black woman of middle age dressed in the blue uniform of a security guard. She had two teeth missing on the top and one on the bottom. In fact, she was not black at all. Her purple-hued face had something soft and squashed about it, like a plum not yet altogether, but almost, turned into a dried prune.

Two seats away from me sat a black man of late middle age, wearing a cap made of a cut-off women's nylon stocking, through the weave of which several stubborn, stiff, white hairs reared like weed through a net. He wasn't really black either, but rather a weather-beaten smoky gray. He kept his eyes half-closed, as if squinting in a glaring light, though the subway car was not particularly well lit. His head was bowed forward, his shoulders somewhat stooped. He stared at the floor.

At the next stop, 42nd and Times Square, an old white homeless woman hobbled aboard, shoving a shopping cart heaped full with all her worldly possessions. She muttered quietly to herself, something between a prayer, a cackle and a howl. Her skin color was not, in fact, white, but rather a waxen beige. Her scent was hardly French perfume.

Ruffling his nose, the smoke-gray man slipped over to the seat beside me.

Maybe she noticed, or maybe not. The homeless woman soon got out again. Whereupon the man breathed an audible sigh of relief.

"You get used to everything," said the woman in the blue uniform. "I know what it means to be homeless. I spent two years in a cardboard box in the Port Authority."

My curiosity aroused, I looked at her as if she were indeed a dried prune come alive.

"Drugs. Crack. My own fault," she answered my gaze.

The man nodded. "That shit is powerful."

"Now I can afford a room, thank God!"

"How did you survive the storm?" I asked the man.

"In prison you at least stay high and dry," he replied. "Just got out. After 31 years everything looks different." A little while later he lifted his head and looked me in the eye, as if in answer to an unasked question. "Murder," he muttered. "Two concurrent life sentences. I was a hitman, a contract killer."

The purple-faced woman in the blue uniform and I went pale. Both of us stared at him with fear and curiosity.

"I studied the law books…found a loophole in the law."

Words failed me.

But he clearly relished the opportunity to speak. His smoke-gray face turned somewhat red, as if he still saw the judge seated before him, he continued. "Guilty – I admit it. Thirty-one years is enough time to think about yourself. But in the meantime everything done changed. It's like I was locked up in New York and let out in a strange city."

There's so much I would have liked to have asked that curious Rip van Winkle. If he experienced space and time differently? Or enticed by an uncertain future, did he stay stuck in the past? Is he still seething with anger? How do things stand with love of his fellow man and regret? In light of his former profession, I didn't dare pose any unwelcome questions, didn't want to upset him.

At 125th Street, without a word, he suddenly got up, got out, and disappeared in the throng.

The woman in blue kept looking after me: "Never would have guessed it!"

And when she, who had lived for two years in a cardboard box, got up at the next stop and stepped out onto the platform, she kept shaking her head.

I peered after her with a certain longing, since I was now the last one left. And then when the doors slid shut with a hefty smack, and with a slow hiss the train set itself in motion, I fell back in a fright at the sight of a color-less, transparent face reflected in the scratched, filthy glass pane of the door, until I suddenly recognized it as my own.

The Bullfighter and the Samurai, a Sports Fairy Tale

I must confess from the start that I have never until now felt any particular fondness, as spectator or participant, for the sport of baseball. It meant nothing more to me than an optimally hard slam with a wooden bat at a round object hurled by another as swiftly as possible in the batter's direction, whereupon all present, that is to say those players dressed in the same colored uniform and the half of the spectators gathered in the stands inclined to favor them, cheer, while the players decked out in the otherwise tinted pants, caps and shirts of the pitcher's team and the other half of the spectators in the stands committed to them either remain silent or else howl and hiss as the batter runs around a freshly cut green field in which nothing but dust and sweat is ever harvested.

Like I said, I felt no affinity for and had no understanding of baseball until one day a houseguest, a diehard baseball fan, insisted on watching the World Series on my T.V. and I, in part out of a certain curiosity, but above all for politeness sake and because on that particular evening

I had nothing better to do, watched along with her. Even the very term "World Series" seemed a bit absurd to me, since although Fidel Castro is and the late Hugo Chavez was apparently also among many diehard fans, it is after all a contest exclusively played between American and a handful of Canadian teams.

It was the second game of the World Series in the new Yankee Stadium in New York, on October 29, 2009, a contest between the New York Yankees and the Philadelphia Phillies. One after the other, stiff-limbed batters marched forth out of the Yankee dugout. Like cows they chewed chewing gum or tobacco with their slowly rising and falling jaws, spit the stuff out with a vulgar slurp, wiped the sweat off their paws onto the seams of their pants and took position with outstretched behind and raised bat at the square-shaped, white home plate, until, one after another, they were swept away like flies by a seasoned 38-year-old pitcher for Philadelphia.

The pitcher, a certain Pedro Martinez, who called himself an old goat, did not come from Philadelphia, but rather from the Dominican Republic, where as a poor boy he practiced pitching with balled-up old socks until he could fling that thing so precisely that he never missed. Now he stood there in quiet anticipation like a proud bullfighter on the white spot in the middle of the field, the pitcher's mound. Meanwhile the majority of the spectators, most of them Yankees fans, greeted him with hisses and curses, because he had beaten their team in the first game of the World Series. And in this second game he had already eliminated three batters, including the famous Alex Rodriguez, aka A-rod, who had recently had a love affair with Madonna, a fleeting reminder of Joe DiMaggio and Marilyn Monroe. Pedro Martinez stood there gazing at the enemy mob with pluck and a hint of disdain, as if to say: "Is that all you've got?"

It's the beginning of the sixth inning. Now the left-handed, 35-year-old Yankee batter Hideki Matsui, known as "Godzilla," a native of Japan, steps up to the plate. His nickname was originally a derisive moniker given on account of a skin condition, subsequently elevated to honorific on account of his skill with the bat. Matsui doesn't chew or spit, just coolly raises his bat and quietly looks his opponent in the eye, like a brave Samurai.

Martinez looks back, immediately fathoms with an almost imperceptible twitch that he has met his match.

And suddenly the whole game becomes a duel. The stadium falls still. Nothing else matters but these two men. One can sense in this encounter the concentrated dignity of two cultures, the Spanish and the Japanese, each embodied by an individual, pitted against each other. The two men appear titanic and mighty, even though both are actually rather small for professional players. The concentration in their clear, crossed looks almost flickers as though with an electromagnetic current. There is no more before and after, only now.

Martinez raises his pitching arm and hurls the ball as swiftly as a thought. Matsui responds, meets the pitch and slams it back. The ball traces a resplendent arch, the geometric conjunction of two movements, two pathways through life, as it flies into the stands over right field. Dumbfounded, albeit impressed, Martinez gazes with quiet awe as Matsui slowly circles the bases with his stiff knees. Martinez almost seems inclined to bow down, partly in grief, partly in joy at having found a worthy opponent. Were Martinez a Samurai he would now, in fact, have to commit hara-kiri. In our culture things are different. Here it's a matter of money, not blood. New York defeated Philadelphia, 3:1. The fans are almost howling for joy.

But such heroic deeds are quickly forgotten. Matsui now plays for Oakland. Martinez has retired. Baseball is still not my thing. But at that moment, in that unforgettable contest between a master pitcher who learned to throw with balled-up socks in Manoguayabo and a master batter with a skin condition and stiff knees from Neagari, Ishikawa, I will admit that today's baseball championships have earned the right to be called World Series.

What Goes Up Must Come Down

Philippe Petit, the latter-day French Houdini famous for an early morning stroll he took in 1974 on a high-wire worthy of the name strung between the soaring twin summits of the World Trade Center, was sentenced at the time by a judge with a sense of humor to "perform" community service in the parks.

I saw him walk a slack rope strung between two trees in Washington Square Park. The impish little pug-nosed man with the slender build of a jockey, the eyes and balance of an eagle—just another acrobat, I thought—was warming up, riding a unicycle around the rim of a chalk circle, before ascending the rope, with a beatific smile and astounding sure-footedness. I will never forget the sudden look of profound displeasure that gripped his beady blue eyes and twisted his thin lips, when, despite his mimed insistence that the throng of spectators stand clear, one hapless sandal-clad miscreant had the audacity to toe the line, and worse, to drop a cigarette butt inside the chalked perimeter. Perfectly balanced, the unicycle stopped dead on an invisible dime, as vexation welled into disgust. Singed by the laser-like intensity of that disapproving sneer, with all eyes upon him, the owner of the offending toes retracted them forthwith, stooped to retrieve the cigarette butt, and slunk off, whereupon Petit went about his business.

The second time I saw him, a few years later, he was walking with a woman I assumed to be his wife, wheeling his offspring, a petite Petit in a pram, a mere mortal making his mundane way along the Avenue of the Americas, his downcast gaze trying to deflect the woman's displeasure and elude the attention of passersby, apparently in the throes of a domestic spat. How else to explain what happened?

The fearless funambulist lionized for having tiptoed across tightropes in the sky, and who would take his act from the World Trade Center to Sydney Harbour Bridge, the Louisiana Superdome, the concourse of Grand Central Station, and a wire stretched across the Seine from the Palais de Chaillot to the second story of the Eiffel Tower, in each locale carefully calibrating wind shifts and weather conditions, miscalculated and proceeded to stumble on a crack, one of those buckled welts endemic to New York sidewalks, and went flying flat on his face.

The *I* of the Tiger

Tyger, tyger, burning bright,
In the forests of the night:
What immortal hand or eye,
Could frame thy fearful symmetry?

William Blake

For years he sailed around the city, his effigy an urban fixture beaming from the side of a bus, the prototypical comic book superhero, blond, blue-eyed and brawny, toying with the tail of a snarling tiger wrapped around his neck. The late Günther Gebel-Williams, wild animal trainer extraordinaire and star of the Ringling Brothers and Barnum and Bailey Circus, a three-time winner of the Ernst Renz Plaque Award, the Oscar of the circus world, proved no less formidable in the flesh, only more human. We talked in a trailer behind the scenes in Madison Square Garden between shows toward the end of his last tour, circa 1978.

«When I come out of the cage»—he holds forth in rapid-fire, German-accented circus English, his hands and eyes punctuating the flow—"many people say: Oh, you not so big! Then I say: Yes, I grow in there, you know, my personality grows in the cage.» No fake bravado. None of that old-time lion tamer stuff for him. «Before, Clyde Beatty...hip hip...bang bang...with pistol and chair»—his tone now mock inflated, with a click of the tongue and a swish of the arm he mimics the crack of the whip—"Oh man!..What I do looks too easy maybe?»

Easy!?

Consider his entrance. Houselights dimmed, the band strikes up a cavalry charge. In the arm of the spotlight a dazzling black sequined figure comes riding out, balanced on the back of an elephant, sharing his maharajah-sized saddle with a Bengal tiger on a leash. It's Tarzan, Hopalong Cassidy, Tonto and the Lone Ranger all rolled into one.

Kill the lights! The band strikes up the theme song from *Chariots of Fire*.

Cut to the cage. There in the artificial sunrise he stands alone, as in the beginning: Adam in Eden.

Enter nineteen tigers.

With the confident ease of a seasoned choreographer, Günther gestures and commands. Each cat heads straight for its assigned place—teachers take note! The whip in his right hand is seldom cracked and seems to serve solely as an extension of his arm. With generous pats and caresses and an occasional stern word only when needed, the master guides his feline ballerinas through their pirouettes and pas de deux. They jump, rear up, roll over, play sideways leapfrog, and a fearsome game of chicken through a flaming hoop.

Class dismissed.

All except for the star cat who props her savage paws on his shoulders and together they waltz around the cage.

It does all look so deceptively easy. Just a bunch of well behaved, five-hundred-pound housecats horsing around. No big deal. Still the three hundred stitches all over his body attest to the difference between waltzing with a calico and a tiger.

As the dance master himself is quick to point out, these «little accidents» were the consequence of trying to break up fights between his pupils, never of a premeditated attack. «When something goes wrong in the cage, I blame myself and ask myself: What did *I* do wrong? I have always to think ahead of them, to guess what they will do next. I want my animals free in their thoughts. I train them to work alone and to think for themselves. I try to let each be herself. It takes a little longer, but it is better for both of us like that.»

"A little longer" means up to two years to finish a single act.

"First I want friendship." (It's easy to forget the man is talking about tigers!) "Two months to make contact. Every day I go to them...Hi hi...sniff sniff...gra gra ...so that soon when they see me, they say: Ah, it's him!...And then I step into their cage...and I let them come out and run loose in the big cage till they feel at home there."

"And then I must overstep the friendship. Let them know: I am not only your friend, but also the boss! Because all the time: Oh, *mein* little pussycat!—that won't get us anywhere...Inside and outside the ring are two separate places."

He first felt the thrill of the ring at age 12, when his mother took him to see the famous Circus Williams performing in Munich at the time. The year was 1946. His father, a soldier, had never returned from the Russian Front. Mother and son had fled westward from their village, Schweinitz, in Silesia (today part of Poland) into the interior of occupied Germany. She found work as a seamstress with the circus, but left after a month, couldn't stand the hectic life. Her son stuck around. He was immediately hooked. Straining for words, he recalled his first impression: "Something... *wunderbar... fantastisch*!...Another world!...Another world!...I go in and never come out again."

"Like a dream?"

"*Some* dream!" Günther shrugs. "Thirty years, never time for anything. Work! Work! Never time for family. Never vacation. Nothing."

"Any regrets?"

"Not for me, no—maybe for my family." (His wife, Sigrid, and daughter, Tine, both tightbodied beauties, and his spunky son, Buffy, are all circus performers, part of the act.) "I myself never felt I was missing anything. I have a job where other people have a hobby. The animals are my life and livelihood. Work...work...always nervous, afraid for what might happen..."

"Afraid for yourself?"

"For me? No! I just don't want anything to happen to my children…and my animals. But for me, nerves of steel!" he winks, parodying the part.

"Always?"

"I don't know…I guess everybody…sometime…but…," he falters before cracking an internal whip. "I'm fast, no time to be afraid…Pang!" (That's him leaping into the cage.) "Vvvvrrraaahhh!" (That's the tigers greeting.) "Either you say: Tiger out, and never again! Or: Let's go, pussycats!"

"Have the animals taught you anything about yourself over the years?"

"Yes, I learn always to be same person, never up and down …always steady…always keep control."

"Control of the wild animal in *you*?"

"Discipline, yes," he deflects the question, bringing the mystery back down to earth, "you cannot be sloppy yourself and expect animals to be correct."

"How do you become a tiger trainer?"

"You learn with your eyes. You stand behind me and watch what I do. And everything I do, you do."

"Did you have a special affinity for animals as a child?"

"Yes, I was always with horses…since ten…never played with other children…only horses. But I never dreamt of the circus then. I wanted to be an engineer."

"Do you ever dream of the animals these days?"

"No, thank God, I'm too tired!"

He tells the story of a bear trainer of his acquaintance who had raised his bears from cubs, thought he knew them inside out. Till one day they lunged for his legs. Almost had to have them amputated. He tried to go on working, but woke up one night in a cold sweat. He had dreamt of his bears. Then he knew it was time to sell them and try something else.

"I only dream about my wife," Günther grins.

He is dressing now for the second half of the show. The part in which he wraps the leopard around his neck, followed by the little number in which he commands a herd of elephants with the sound of his voice, makes them sit down, spin around and rear up, Radio City Rockettes-style, with their front legs poised on each other's rumps. One graceful mastodon dances around holding a tambourine with its trunk, smacking it against a pillar-like leg. Another tips forward and stands on its head. And for his grand finale, Günther has an elephant charge at him and stamp on a seesaw, sending him flying in a backwards somersault up onto the shoulders of another patiently waiting mammoth.

"Five minutes!" Sigrid bursts in.

"Why do people keep coming to the circus? What's the attraction?" I ask.

«The last clean entertainment,» his minimally attired

wife suggests, «no violence, no sex.»

I nod politely, thinking there's nothing sexier than a high wire act in a scant bikini and nothing more on the verge of violence than a man alone with a tiger in a cage—a scene that harkens back to the bloody antique spectacle from which the circus gets its name. But circus sex and violence are a sustained suggestive wink at what *might* happen, more tease than titillation.

Time for one last question: "What do spectators see in your act? Is it the primeval memory of a time when man lived closer to animals?"

"Maybe…I think…" he pauses, on the edge of some existential revelation, but the band is already striking up his entrance.

"I know," says Sigrid, "he's the last great American hero."

"Bullshit!" Günther shakes his head and rushes off to the ring.

Love thy Neighbor

Neighbors are an urban anomaly, resolute strangers whose parallel lives are separated by a wall, a hallway or a flight of stairs, insulating them against intimacy. Nowhere is this more true than in New York, where a bilateral façade of civility is maintained by nods, smiles, non-committal words of greeting, banal exchanges on the weather, and plumbing problems, until one day an incident pierces the divide and risks disrupting privacy, that most prized commodity in the cramped ant hill of eight and a half million.

Try as you might to hide, high rises disseminate the telling odors of diverse domesticities; anything roasting, stewing, steaming, or boiling in or on the ovens or hearts of its inhabitants inevitably spills over into the hallway. It is embarrassing to sniff these private smells in passing. You know what your neighbors are eating and what's eating them. Having grown up in a private house, I am often overcome by a sudden terror at the thought of the walls giving way and the ceiling caving in, and all those destinies literally dropping in.

1.

THE RESTORER OF ICONS

I first met Kiril when his knees buckled under.

"Pleased very much to meet you," he said with a Slavic accent and a certain formality when I found him collapsed at my door.

"The pleasure is all mine," I replied, hoisting him upright, and conveying him home to his flat on the floor above mine. The falls repeated themselves, as did the ritual uplifting, whereupon a semblance of friendship ensued.

"I'm 96, going on eternity!" he winked an eye as blue as a glacial lake. Slender, with a wrinkle-free face on which the years had put a golden patina, his hair was white as a fresh snowfall in a virgin forest. A restorer of icons by trade, Kiril had holed up for more than a quarter century, the longest time he had ever lived in any one place, with his elfin wife, Natalia, in their cramped one-bedroom apartment, the walls of which were covered with blue-eyed Slavic saints that might well have doubled as Kiril's cousins.

"It's been a long winter," I remarked, "must remind you of Russia."

"Oh no," he ruffled his porcelain-like heirloom of a nose in disgust, "New York snow has no *veshchestvo*, no substance!"

He had, he told me, led a life of repeated displacements,

a compact history of the 20th century.

Fleeing the Russian Revolution from St. Petersburg to Prague; to Berlin, where a family friend, the statesman Vladimir Dmitrievich Nabokov, father of the noted novelist and lepidopterist, was mistakenly felled before his eyes by an assassin's bullet meant for someone else; to wartime Paris and the provinces, where the family was hosted in crumbling châteaux by gracious, albeit destitute, members of the French aristocracy who generously shared their subsistence diet of boiled potatoes and vintage Bordeaux, the potato skins saved and fed to a single pig fattened up for Christmas, the empty bottles scattered about to catch the rain leaking in through the roof they could not afford to fix; to Peron's Buenos Aires, where the quiet, well-mannered young Spaniard, a certain Ramón Mercader, who boarded with them for a while to help them make ends meet, later turned up on the front page of the paper as Leon Trotsky's assassin—Natalia and he finally ended up in New York, always assuming it would be temporary.

Memory had pickled his intimates and past acquaintances into the characters of a Russian novel Kiril sincerely hoped I would help him write, which—as he later confessed—was his ulterior motive for collapsing at my front door upon hearing the tap of my typewriter keys. (This was a good two decades before the discrete click of the word processor.) His great uncle, an impeccably dressed dandy who drank champagne for breakfast and kept a dose of strychnine in the hollowed-out ivory handle of his cane for unforeseen circumstances on the eve of the

Revolution, had been—Kiril let slip—Dostoyevsky's last publisher, the lure of whose posthumous literary pedigree was no doubt meant to tempt me to take on the onerous project. His real life heroine, Natalia, daughter of a wealthy boyar, forsook her father's estate to run off with a penniless icon painter of noble blood, fortuitously, as it turned out, the day before the local peasantry set fire to the family manor. Natalia's once golden blonde, now ermine white, tightly braided mane, would, if unwound—Kiril boasted with a wink—"stretch the width of Nevsky Prospect, or Broadway, take your pick."

Each visit began with steaming hot tea poured from a samovar and ended with chilled vodka. "The first glass oils *la gorge*," Kiril demonstrated, flinging his head back, downing its contents in a devil-may-care gulp. "The second stirs the craving for more. The third glass makes lips tremble like virgin bride at first kiss. After fourth glass…who's counting?"

The icons blinked. But Natalia prudently gathered up the precious crystal glasses, corked the bottle and showed me to the door before Kiril could get carried away and the novel ever got written.

2 .

THE ROCKETTE

"Midnight! Midnight!"

How many times was I awakened from insomniac unrest by what sounded like a fairy queen casting a spell in the dead of night, but proved instead to be my downstairs neighbor Joanne vainly, desperately, calling her black tomcat home from a night's prowl.

A former Radio City Music Hall Rockette, Joanne still had a dancer's legs, though arthritis gnawed at the knees and varicose veins crisscrossed her calves like an intricate stocking pattern. Deaf and limping, her once long blonde locks faded white, face caked with a cosmetic mask of make-up and powder, it was difficult to imagine her kicking in concert across the stage with a bevy of scantily clad beauties stirring the libidos of repressed suburbanites out on the town with their toddlers and the Missus in tow.

Whenever we crossed paths on the creaking stairwell that sometimes sounded like the stacked keys of an out-of-tune player piano, sometimes like a broken accordion, and sometimes like the wheezing gills of a dying fish, Joanne gave the impression of a wizened, wobbly Blanche DuBois. Having long since lost her trust in the kindness of strangers, she lived with an ever multiplying menagerie of stray cats and dogs. The stench and din reached such proportions that Theodore, the aging Greek hairdresser who ran a beauty salon, in the back room of which he lived on the first floor, directly below her, circulated a petition to have her expelled for health code violations, and when I refused to sign, called me a coward.

Joanne emerged ever more infrequently after that, accompanied on those rare occasions when we met by a cacophony of barks and yowls and the pungent stench of animal feces which she vainly attempted to camou-flage with air freshener, cheap cologne, and ear-tingling screams.

One day I found her doubled over on her hands and knees, rummaging through the contents of toppled trash cans at the foot of the stairs.

"I lost it!" she wailed.

"What did you lose, Joanne?"

Beside herself, sobbing, it took her a while to find the words.

Convinced that her eviction was imminent, in a vain attempt to make the place more presentable for an impending visit of the health inspectors, ASPCA et al., she had inadvertently tossed out her prized possession, a black and white publicity headshot of the comedian Lenny Bruce, signed: "I'd give it all up for those legs! Love, Lenny."

3.

THE MERCHANT MARINE

Directly across the hall lived Ellen, a merchant marine. Ellen was a walking, talking United Nations with her arched unibrow and the trace of a mustache à la Frieda Kahlo, with a prickly tenacity to her long black Cherokee hair, and the expression of her Eurasian eyes forever fluctuating between soulful, sultry and soused. She had multiple personalities which she juggled like an acrobat.

There was Ellen the female rover who had spent a lifetime sailing the seven seas.

And fearless Ellen, who once, on a bet, dressed up in a man's burnoose to pass, untroubled, through the fabled Kasbah in Casablanca.

Wistful Ellen, whose one true love was knifed to death and dumped overboard in a drug deal gone bad in the Panama Canal, over whom she still wept.

Faithful Ellen, who claimed she could never love again, but that didn't keep her from trying.

Kind Ellen, who knocked at my door with a heaping plate of rice and beans or whatever she was cooking.

Superstitious Ellen, who kept a Christian crucifix, a Muslim hand of Fatima, a Jewish mezuzah, and a Haitian voodoo doll dangling from her doorpost to ward off all attendant spirits and put heaven on her side, because you never know.

Tough broad Ellen, who once in a drunken frenzy heaved a fist through the plate glass door downstairs to let herself in, having forgotten her keys.

Careless Ellen, who kept five fans running one hot summer night, went out for a drink, or two or three, and in her absence, fanned up the flames of an electrical fire that almost burnt down the house—inspiring the Rock 'n' Roll memorabilia shop that replaced the hairdresser downstairs, whose manager snapped a picture of the flames pouring out of her window, and had the image printed on a calling card, dubbing their digs "the hottest place in town"— cremating her pet poodle Princess in the process.

Disheveled Ellen, who greeted me dead drunk at the head of the stairs with a kiss on the lips and a hint of an invitation I might once have welcomed way back when, but respectfully declined the night before she retired to Florida.

4.

THE MOUSE

Not all neighbors pay rent.

A mouse moved in one day. I never actually saw it eye to eye, though I did occasionally hear it swishing about at night. I set a trap, and baited it on Ellen's advice, with bacon, rather than the proverbial hunk of cheese. It neither surprised nor upset me that though the bacon was gone the next morning, snatched out from under the deadly metal jaw, the mouse escaped unscathed. I reset the trap several times, but the result was always the same, so I quit trying to trap it.

My attitude changed over time, my initial revulsion evolving, first, into a mild displeasure, and thereafter leveling off from reluctant indulgence into a live-and-let-live attitude that grew in time into a grudging admiration. I won't pretend that I ever actually became fond of its presence, as people do with their pets, but let's just say the creature's perambulations ceased to matter. I simply did not want to be bothered and soon forgot about it.

It was many months, maybe a year, later that I became aware of a certain smell. At first I thought it emanated from Joanne's place downstairs, or possibly from the Rock 'n' Roll memorabilia emporium where they threw wild parties and did various recreational drugs. I myself am admittedly not the most assiduous of housekeepers: papers pile up, crumbs fall where they may, dust tends to gather like dried up and condensed snow drifts, and I am even reticent to swish away spider webs, and tend rather to let them dangle from the ceiling like withered trellises left over from last year's new year's eve celebration.

I cannot quite describe the smell except to suggest that its pungency was neither altogether disagreeable nor enticing. The longer I lived with it the more my nostrils became acclimatized, the way we become to bodily odors, like that of underarm sweat, for instance, which we find repulsive in others, but strangely comforting in ourselves. In time, however, the odor ripened into that of a strong cheese. And anyone who knows me knows that I cannot abide the odor of cheese. And so I began to hunt for its source.

My search was haphazard at first. But when such carelessness failed to locate the culprit, the search turned more systematic, obsessive, maniacal. The odor soon occupied my entire consciousness, and all I could think about was to track it down, discover and eliminate its source. But life goes on and even the most stubborn obsession recedes in imminence, successively replaced by other more pressing annoyances. Either my sensitivity to it diminished or the odor itself faded.

It was not long after I gave up the hunt that I stumbled upon an extraordinary find while rummaging through a stash of papers shoved into a closet. Shriveled up, but unmistakable in structure from tail to snout was the mummy of a mouse, its tiny teeth clamped shut, as if on a choice tidbit, which had since disintegrated, its dried lips curled into the semblance of a smile.

On Foot

On several occasions and on different continents I happened upon a man who was walking around the world.

The first time, I spotted him on a highway in the mountains north of Castellón in Spain where I had gone to visit the cave paintings. A trucker offered me a lift to my destination from the desolate *Plaza Major* of a tiny market town whose name I can't recall, the last stop on the municipal bus line, where a busload of chickens and I had been dropped off at dawn. He would in any case be hauling the chickens to slaughter, he indicated with a grin in their direction and a hand to his throat, and there was room up front for me.

As I spoke next to no Spanish, and he no English, communication between us was elemental, to say the least. He would point at something or other, the sky or the state of the road, and I would nod, while the chickens kept up their cackling commentary. It was a cold sunny day in February. Drowsy, I rolled the window down a crack and a whisper of wind pleasantly fanned my bleary eyes as we drove along. I was about to drift off to sleep when suddenly an object thumped hard against the front of the truck. It sounded like a stone. The trucker calmly hit the brakes, climbed out and soon returned with a sparrow lying still in the palm of his hand, its little body steaming, blood trickling from its beak.

The bird had flown straight into the radiator and so found death on contact. The chickens must have gotten the scent, for they let out a fearsome squall. Even I understand the chicken word for death. And just then, as we were about to set out again, an old man with a staff came walking along.

Though I could not follow the words precisely, the gist of their interchange was clear.

Would the old man like a lift?

No, thank you!

But it's quite a hike to *Morella*!

The old man shook his head again and walked on, a solitary profile, stooped and vulnerable against the vastness of nature.

Where was he coming from? Where was he headed? I wondered. And the trucker, still holding the dead bird in his hand, wondered too. Glancing from the old man (a distant ridiculous stick figure now) to the bird, to me, he shook his head.

No doubt about it, he and I both sensed something out of the ordinary. And though the trucker was definitely not given to metaphysical musings or excessive sentiment– he tossed the dead bird out the window like a handful of garbage and wiped the blood on his pants leg—yet he had, I could tell by the glazed look in his eyes, been moved by the tiny tragedy of the bird and the stubborn endurance of the old man.

The trucker shook his head again, this time I think to clean the slate, to put the inexplicable out of his mind before stepping on the gas.

We continued our journey without any further incident.

And when finally I reached my destination, following a hasty hike at sunset with an innkeeper who doubled as guide and his dog, the dog barked and the man pointed to an overhanging canopy of rock. At first I saw nothing, but the dog kept barking and my guide beckoned me to step closer. There was the unmistakable image of a stick figure silhouetted against the sun, slightly stooped, his legs spread, suggesting motion, a staff in hand, and a bird hovering overhead.

When next we crossed paths in time and space, he or someone very much like him had jumped continents to the mountains of North Carolina—which state I happened to be speeding through in the company of a friend, whose grandmother lay dying in a nursing home in Georgia. It was a hot spring day. I idly let my hand hang out the window and skim the air like a bird, when I spotted an old man with a walking stick. His clothes were different, but his stoop and his determined stride immediately brought that other pedestrian to mind. My friend noticed him too in the rearview mirror, and must have likewise been struck by something in his mien–or maybe she was just thinking of her grandma–: she hit the brakes, pulled over and waited for him to catch up with the car.

"Can I give you a lift, old man?" she asked.

He shook his head and kept on walking.

If it was the same man—and I'm not saying for certain that it was, only that it might have been—he must have heard the same question repeated in every conceivable language, posed by people in passing cars and trucks, ox-carts and rickshaws. And though the sounds varied, the sequence of response was the same. Always a brusque refusal, met by the same puzzled look on the face of the would-be benefactor: a composite of confusion, reverence, envy and the anger we feel for that which we do not understand. That proud and resolute shake of the head appeared at once so saintly and stupid, which may after all be much the same.

One more occasion bears mention.

I had been hitchhiking through the State of Washington—or was it Oregon?—I can't now recall the exact circumstances, the season or the time of day. All that I remember distinctly is the battered black Thunderbird, and the fact that the driver had a scar across his throat from ear to ear and drove too quickly. When he dented the metal railing at a hairpin curve and skidded uncomfortably close to the precipice, I wanted out.

Marooned on foot where nowhere meets the horizon, one moment my legs were shaking, leaden with terror, and the next moment—it was as in a dream in which the dreamer can no longer distinguish between himself and his surroundings. The sun winked. The road curled underfoot like a cat caressed, its supple asphalt spine arching upwards to meet my every step. And then I remembered the old man and understood in a flash his refusal to accept a ride.

But a little later, when a red convertible skidded to a halt in a cloud of dust and gravel, and the door swung open, and a beautiful black woman sleek as a bird lifted her sunglasses, looked me over with a languid smile, said she was tired of driving—What else could I do!—I went weak in the knees and climbed in.

IV

Wise Cracks

THIS
AS MAD

Rockefeller
Brothers Fund
Philanthropy for an Interdependent W

Elsewhere in Eden

Elsewhere in Eden an androgynous tree blossomed. The fruit bit the man. The man bit the woman. She howled and gave birth to a snake.

Rough Cuts

1

Today the surgeon cut a little cancer out of me, a parcel of myself that had grown wild and threatened to consume the rest. Hair has that tendency too if left to its own devices. Barber and surgeon are historically related at the root. Only the instruments have changed. Cut it out, you insist, cancer is no laughing matter. Cancer kills you if you don't uproot it. It's a kind of shoot-out at the O.K. Corral, the surgeon a high-paid gunslinger, or rather knife wielder, hired to have it out with my renegade cells.

Now this particular cancer happened to grow on my right forearm, a nasty place for any right-handed person, all the more so for a writer.

"Easy does it, nothing to it," remarked the surgeon with a certain swagger no doubt meant to reassure the patient. "If you had to pick a cancer from a catalogue, that's the one you'd want."

Comforted somewhat that the surgeon approved of my selection, I opted for a local anesthetic, wanting to have my wits about me during the procedure.

While cutting, the surgeon kept us both entertained with a wry account of a patient he'd once operated on at Bellevue Hospital, a drunk who'd lost **a** leg after stumbling in between a colliding truck and a taxi, in an accident in which the taxi driver also lost a leg. The drunk's no less inebriated buddies sent him directly to the hospital in an ambulance and dutifully followed in a cab, clutching the severed limb which they'd managed to salvage from the wreckage before the crashed vehicles burst into flames. Only when they got to the hospital, the surgeon pointed out to them that they'd plucked the wrong leg out of the wreckage, and that, henceforth, their friend would hobble through life on two left legs.

Apocryphal perhaps, he made the story last as long as the cutting. "I just love to cut!" the surgeon shook his head with a wistful sigh, evidently disappointed that it was already over and done with.

I myself was relieved. "If you had to pick a talent from the catalogue," I said, "that's the one *I*'d want *you* to have!"

For the stitching, he told me of an old Greenwich Village character, a poet with no health insurance, who paid for each operation with a poem. "I remember one about a pair of surgical scissors, but don't ask me to recite it," he said, "mnemonics is not one of my strengths."

"I'm from The Village too," I said.

"No poems, please," he said, "you pay."

Fortunately I had insurance. My only regret was not to have taken a parting glimpse at the piece of me he cut out.

In a grudging way I admired the cancer for its stubborn will to grow, its total lack of concern for the surrounding cells comprising the rest of me. If only we could harness such pig-headed resolve to grow parts of ourselves on demand. In my case, I wouldn't mind adding an inch or two at the top and trimming the same round the middle. From Nature's perspective, I suppose, humanity is one big hungry tumor growing wildly beyond its allotted slot, colonizing, conquering, consuming.

Think I'll go get a haircut.

2

Staring down at the heap of fleece on the floor after a haircut, I have always suffered a pang of separation as if from a disposable accumulation of self. And when lifting what's left of me out of the barber chair, I wobble a bit, feeling out the lightness and the loss.

Haircuts have always been traumatic.

Once, while I was in the hot seat at the barbershop of my early boyhood, a black limousine pulled up and a man with a black Fedora stepped out. Not given to undue haste, Giuseppe, who had just about finished my right side, ran to hold the door. "A trim," said the man, removing his black Fedora, revealing a more or less bald pate with a white fuzz round the ears. Making a big to do over every strand, Giuseppe kept trembling after the man had gone. My mother had to remind him to attend to the left side of my head.

In late adolescence, I tried a barber school. With their hair slicked back and glittering gold teeth, the barbers-in-training looked like hungry young sharks, but having entered their precinct I was too intimidated to escape. Nodding at my request for a parting on the left, my trainee, who had been trimming his nose hairs, reached for an electric sheer and proceeded to take it all off, military-style.

"What about the parting?" I asked, straining to hold back the tears.

He shook his head and shrugged: "Too short!"

There were those years, following the arrival of the Beatles, when having it cut meant capitulation to the fleece police, lean years for the trade.

Various girlfriends subsequently had a go at it, but the Samson and Delilah thing and a few mistakes prompted me to return to professionals.

Vincent, my current cutter, likes to talk about the plot of land he owns in Upstate New York. He can close his eyes, he claims, and picture every wild flower and weed. I figure a man who respects things that grow will go easy on the wispy boundary between being and nothingness.

Conversing with my reflection in the mirror—as tenuous a part of me as the falling locks—Vincent tells tales of the trade: what hairdos Madonna used to have done before she made it, and how the playwright Miguel Piñero dropped by one day before presenting his first script to the impresario Joseph Papp. "Lighten me up for luck!" he said. Papp took the play and put Piñero on the map. Vincent has not yet performed such miracles for me, but I'm a patient man and consider each haircut a high-risk investment.

Keys

My wife objects to my keeping old keys to long forsaken alcoves of the past. Loading down the key ring and stuffing out my pants pocket, as they do, I might well be mistaken for a security guard, a realtor, or a jailor. There are rings attached to rings, each affixed with keys of every kind, paracentric, internal cut, dimple, and tubular. But I take comfort in their muffled music whenever I reach in to feel the metal. I can read them as a blind man might. Running my index finger along the notched rim, I can unlock imagined doors.

There are the keys to known locales: my apartment, the studio in which I write, my office, the empty house in which I grew up, the lock to the black English racing bike in a storeroom in the basement that I haven't ridden for decades. I can hear the distinctive click of each lock and the idiosyncratic squeak of each door. The impression is powerful enough to trigger a precise olfactory memory of the musty or oily scent of first entry and crystallize the absence into a presence.

And then there are the keys to the forgotten locks of doors I don't remember. My wife is right. There's no logical reason to keep them, except for the lingering whimsy that maybe, just maybe, wherever it is, should I stumble upon it by happenstance or animal instinct, I might feel inclined to reenter someday. No doubt the locks have long since been changed, even if I could remember where the doorways were, and the rooms to which they once lent access are inhabited by strangers who, in turn, took over from other strangers, each filling the once familiar space with their own suffocating mix of loneliness and intimacy, none of whom would have the slightest interest in my tenuous attachment, and would rightfully be suspicious should I seek entry.

I remember a movie called *The Key* starring William Holden and Sophia Loren, about a sailor who, in a storm at sea, is handed a key to an apartment in an unspecified port by a fellow mariner with an inkling of his doom. I cannot swear to the specifics of the plot. But I do remember a breathless Holden turning the key in a lock, only to find a somewhat disconcerted, albeit luscious looking, Loren waiting within. No idea just what she was doing there, only that she had on a tight dress and was attached by an unspecified arrangement to the bearer of that key.

It's not that I'm planning any infidelities. It's that a key, whatever key, is a powerful metaphor of access. Alice is tantalized by keys, locks and doorways of fluctuating size in Wonderland. St. Peter famously clutches the keys to heaven, though the traditional depiction of angels ceaselessly strumming on lutes to which the blessed dance hardly seems all that enticing.

The plastic passkeys in modern hotel rooms don't quite do it for me either. A red light goes green, signaling go, but the metal click is missing, and my imagination is just not aroused at the prospect of advancing at the green light and metaphorically stepping out onto the roadbed with motorists and truckers watching me undress. I have occasionally forgotten to return such plastic keys at checkout, suddenly discovering them stuffed among receipts in my shirt pocket, but the discovery leaves me cold. Those soulless cards lack the tactile enticement of metal. My virtual return already a programmed impossibility, I have never even contemplated saving one as a souvenir.

No doubt my attachment to notched blades and matching tumblers harkens back to the Gothic, haunted houses, graveyards and the like. For keys do indeed give off a frisson, though I would not necessarily call it fear. The emotions stirred up are rather akin to loss and longing. Every key is a kind of mnemonic Madeleine, its jingle the elusive theme song of my own *à la recherche du temps perdu*.

Occasionally, in a fit, I have angrily detached and tossed away a key, hurled it down a disposal chute, through a sewer grating, or into a body of water. But the fleeting relief of having lightened my load, made peace with the past and room for the future, is almost immediately choked back by the ache of the irretrievable. Knowing that that lock to that doorway is eternally closed to me now, I am left with one less option, one less means of retreat, one less pivot or pause on my restless stumble from the womb to the tomb.

A Modest Proposal to Combine Toilet Stalls, Telephone and Voting Booths for Increased Efficiency, Turnout and Satisfaction*

Picture this! It's the day of the local school board elections and they're expecting the same low turnout as always. But wait! What's that? The flow is slow but steady. All day long they've been coming in off the street, eager and ready to cast their ballot, armed with a quarter and recyclable soft weave rolls of campaign literature provided by the candidates and their supporters. The voting time is variable, depending on personal habits, degree of preparedness, diet, and calling pattern. But fluctuations in the norm can be factored

---

* The reader will note certain anachronisms in this essay written and published in 1996. The monopoly of Ma Bell was not yet broken into the smaller entities of AT&T and Verizon, a local phone call still cost a quarter, and the cell phone had not yet rendered the phone booth an extinct species. Voting booths have since been replaced by virtual electronic voting nooks devoid of privacy, in which the sexless scanner replaces the tantalizing downwards thrust of the lever.

into the total for an acceptable average turnout time. The sanitation people are happy. So are the plumbers. Ma Bell's faltering campaign to push public phones has finally paid off. And best of all, civic responsibility is on the rise, a fact which ought to please religious leaders and politicians of every stripe.

The scenario is not as utopian as it might seem and can easily be achieved with a little imaginative urban planning. Indeed, why clutter the schools and public places with those clunky curtained "Porto-Sans" of the electoral season, when the structures you want are already in place and merely require a slight functional modification!

The plan is simple enough. If washing machines come in compact invertible models that double as dryer, radio-alarms can also brew coffee, and fax-phone-answering machines tackle it all, then surely someone could design a multipurpose module to simultaneously satisfy the biological, electoral and telecommunications needs of John and Jane Q. Public.

The idea crystallized, of course, where most of my best ideas do, while seated on the can one day. I was skimming an article on the shrinking participation in national and especially local elections. And being a dedicated voter myself, never having missed a single ballot in the 25 years and counting since my majority, I wondered just what it was that attracted me to the electoral process and turned others off. And just then the telephone rang, as it invariably does at the least opportune moment, and of course, by the time I got around to answering it the caller had hung up.

And then it came to me in a flash, the feature that toilet stalls, voting and telephone booths have in common: that cozy sense of closure. For each is a temporary retreat from the crowd, an oasis of privacy. Why not combine functions and kill three birds with one stone!? So I reached for my pen and scribbled this proposal on the only paper at hand.

Now I may be one of the very few people who feel this way, but voting booths have always given me an erotic tingle. I like to position myself in line so that there's someone worth looking at directly in front of me—in my case, a female, but the same could be true for any sexual proclivity. I take her in from head to toe, let her image imprint itself on my mind, creating a kind of carnal hologram. And when she slips behind the curtain, the effect is that of virtual burlesque. I stare at her legs, wondering how she casts her ballot. Then I think of the things that could conceivably transpire behind that curtain if one were quick and agile enough. And once she pulls back the curtain with a fleeting smile of purpose on her lips and a sigh of satisfaction, I inhale her lingering scent and hold it with me as I, in turn, take her place. The climax comes when after a few moments of reflection on my predecessor's qualities and the candidate's qualifications, I flick a few switches and pull the lever.[*]

---

[*] Here, again, the text shows its age. Manual voting booths have since been replaced by the electronic variety to insure against the phantom hanging chads of the infamous Florida presidential election in 2000.

What, if anything at all, you ask, can this process possibly have in common with the functions effectuated at the loci of long distance and elimination?

Let's start with the public telephone.

You will remember, I trust, the old-fashioned enclosed phone booth in service before they rudely ripped off its folding door in the '70s and shrank it down to the stunted, pathetic, open-backed phone stand of today! Gone the site of Clark Kent's quick change, where the ordinary caller could rent an illusion of intimacy at ten cents a pop! Seated behind a folding glass door, you could ignore the angry minions on line and let your consciousness dissolve locally or long distance. And even the operators with their sultry faceless smirks stirred the libido—Number please!—a far cry from the contemporary computer-generated neuter attacks programmed to intrude every two minutes with the ominous threat to "terminate" call and caller. Inscribed in the vintage wooden panels of old were numbers and names to which a fertile imagination could attach features.

As for the public toilet stall, it has never, of course, been selective in the business of bodily discharge. Relaxed sphincters are a green light for virtual or actual two-way traffic. The white tiles invite an unexpurgated spill-over from the collective well of the unconscious. My all-time favorite inscription on the wall of a café water closet in Rome portrayed three images of an engorged penis, before, during, and after, drawn with Renaissance precision and perspective and captioned with Caesar's famous dictum: *Veni! Vidi! Vici!* (I came! I saw! I conquered!). This, by the way, in a country in which a stripper ran for high public office and almost won. (Okay, so the Italians keep changing governments! Doesn't that prove the popularity of the electoral process?)

Telephone booths attract long lines of would-be callers in all kinds of weather. Toilet stalls are seldom lacking in customers. So why couldn't a voting booth be jazzed up a bit to entice the prospective user? And why indeed, if communication and elimination are proven draws, could they not be combined in locale with electoral politics (especially considering the cathartic effect of casting a ballot and the fact that politics is in any case already associated with the sewer!)? The voting booth would only benefit in activity and, in turn, add cachet and a certain respectability to the seamy side of telephone booths and toilet stalls, the latter often confused with the former?

I would recommend that American Standard, the leading manufacturer of public toilet fixtures in the U.S., design a hybrid unit with a flush in place of a lever and a telephone receiver resting on an Economatic toilet roll dispenser. Or better yet, let each political party provide a competing colorful dispenser with its candidates smiling image imprinted on every sheet. A quarter would suffice to release sufficient quantities of paper, open the phone and ballot line, and revenues could be applied to defray the cost of the campaign. American Standard, whose company name already graces tanks and tiles from coast to coast, would reap the benefits of enhanced public image.

As an added refinement, I would permit the parties to station their cohorts outside the restroom precinct to hand out supplementary rolls of recyclable campaign literature. Furthermore, for a racier effect, I would allow candidates to hire graffiti artists to depict them and their spouses naked. This would permit the voter-caller-eliminator to imagine various forms of intercourse, say, with the prospective President and First Lady before casting his or her ballot (a dimension now already covered by the new media), while dialing 900 for an X-rated political party line immediately prior to pulling the flush-lever. Also, voters would be encouraged to write or draw their candid assessment of the candidates on pressure-sensitive wall panels, thus providing a built-in exit poll.

Place a call, elect a President, eliminate waste—all in a single sitting, on the thunder mug of our great participatory democracy!

I am herewith submitting this proposal on a roll of Scott Tissue to the leadership of the Republican National Committee, whose pronounced anal tendencies and ardent desire to streamline the system make them likely to be more receptive to radical solutions than the Democrats. Who knows, they may even wish to tag it as a rider to their Contract with America!

Confessions of a Tabloid Junkie

Its headlines are classics unto themselves: "SPECIAL NEWS BULLETIN FROM NASA: HEAVEN PHOTOGRAPHED BY HUBBLE TELESCOPE— 'We found where God lives,' says scientist." "SATAN'S FACE IN HURRICANE ANDREW! Evil image appears in storm clouds over Miami!" "Super genius dazzles docs—BOY WITH 2 BRAINS!"

The late Nobel laureate in literature and former U.S. poet laureate, Joseph Brodsky, dreamed of putting poetry in the supermarket. He did not realize, rarely himself perusing the aisles, that poetry in the rough as wild as anything Coleridge ever composed on a pipe-full of opium is right there on the checkout counter rack sandwiched in between scandal and candy.

Not to be confused with *The Star* or *The National Enquirer*, specialists in celebrity smut, the beat covered by the *Weekly World News** is strictly outer limits, extraterrestrial, twilight zone.

---

* The print version, whose circulation once reached 1.2 million, bit the dust in 2007, but the publication was reborn online in 2009.

I still remember the cover that hooked me: "FARMER SHOOTS 24 FOOT GRASSHOPPER!" emblazoned in big bold white caps above the photo of a gawky Norman Rockwellesque yokel in traditional hunter's pose proudly displaying his Herculean prey. The photo retouch may have been a bit primitive back then, but the surreal juxtaposition of seemingly incompatible parts proved strangely compelling, like one of those "pick-out-what-isn't-right-in-this-picture" schoolbook exercises. It brought to mind the brave little tailor of the Brothers Grimm who boasted of bagging seven in a single blow—flies, that is! I chuckled at first, laughed uncomfortably, looked about with an awkward grin, made sure nobody noticed, and stuffed the paper into my bag while the cashier wasn't looking. I was more embarrassed bringing it home than I had been with my first skin magazine.

I buy it now in broad daylight, immune to the smirks of my fellow shoppers. Far from holding the truths it reports to be self-evident, the *Weekly World News* mines the shadow of a doubt: for these are not articles of fact, but articles of faith. We're talking unfiltered legend, freeze-dried nuggets of Myth with a capital M. The archetypes and folk motifs run rampant—Carl Jung would have been in Seventh Heaven, Joseph Campbell on Cloud Nine! Mainlining the American collective unconscious, stories like: "I HAD BIGFOOT'S SON!"…"WEREWOLF BATTLES COPS IN ALABAMA!"…"2-YEAR-OLD'S REINCARNATION OF BETTE DAVIS!—THE PROOF IS IN THE EYES!"…"MIRACLE METEOR

MAKES OLD PEOPLE YOUNG!" out-freak Tod Browning, out-special-effect Spielberg, Lucas & Co., continuing in the great American Dream tradition of Ponce de Leon's and Aunt Sadie's search for the Fountain of Eternal Youth in Florida, where coincidentally, the paper is published.

Take, for instance, the item you might have missed in the dailies a few years back photographically documenting then candidate Bill Clinton's historic handshake with a space alien that helped him clinch his presidential victory (an allegorical allusion to the Arkansan's then way out outsider status); or the revelation of then presidential candidate Bob Dole's skeleton in the closet, the "fact" that his great-grandmother was a bearded dwarf. And where else would you have learned that Dole means penis in Farsi (*WWN*, 5/7/96), the fitting follow-up to Nixon's moniker: Tricky Dick! Like the clowns seated in baseball-primed dunking stalls at state fairs, we want our candidates available for public ridicule before elevating them to high office.

Lest any elitist skepticism prevent you from buying the above, just look at the back of the dollar bill and realize that our economy and culture rock on the iconic fulcrum of a UFO, a green eye hovering in a cloud above an Egyptian pyramid! And did we not once upon a time entrust the fate of the New World Order to Nancy Reagan's astrologer!

We are a nation of frustrated utopians trapped in a never-ending nightmare of consumer craving, epitomized by the *WWN*-exclusive contemporary take on Peter Pumpkin Eater, the "Hubby Who Keeps Dead Wife in A Glass Coffee Table."

Freemen of Montana, Hare Krishnaites, harried commuters, "martyrs" of Waco, suburban housewives, Salt Lake City Mormons, Nation of Islamites and Crown Heights Chassidim, strung-out middle-aged flower children, investment bankers on cocaine, panhandlers on crack, and ordinary desperados like you and I—we're all American Dreamers reluctant to wake up, wanting out of the vacuum of our lives every bit as badly as did the Pilgrims who fled England and landed at Plymouth Rock and the pioneers who kept pushing Westward.

Gospel of the shopping mall, the *Weekly World News* is all we have left of the elusive Wild West! And though the old-tome saints have marched out of commission, the *WWN* regularly adds apocrypha to the All-American hagiographies of our own beloved Saint Elvis, Marilyn, Natalie, and the late beatified Jackie, consort of St. Jack (whose relics recently brought in a pretty penny, as substantiated in the same straight papers that failed to mention another *WWN*-exclusive shocker, that "JFK WAS SHOT TO PREVENT HIM FROM REVEALING – THE TRUTH ABOUT UFOS!") Faithfully reporting all Elvis sightings (including his posthumous nuptial in 1992 to a Mississippi waitress—"Where Elvis and bride are living remains a mystery!), the *WWN* scooped The King's apotheosis into a postage stamp, the ultimate and official canonization of our icons.

Every heaven, of course, needs a Hell to lean on. The same blazing red-covered collector's edition that featured a snapshot of Satan's face in the eye of Hurricane Andrew also revealed the "awesome unknown truth…" (the ultimate misogynist fantasy) that the modern day Prince of Evil, "ADOLF HITLER WAS A WOMAN." If you can't beat 'em, demonize 'em! Precedents abound in American tradition, notably the witches of Salem.

The improvisational range and imaginative daring of *WWN* editors is truly mind-boggling! There's the wife that hasn't showered since seeing the movie Psycho, the space alien belief that "EARTH IS A BAD NEIGHBOR-HOOD!—That's why they seldom land!" top scientists say; vampire hijackings of bloodmobiles; a handwritten invitation to The Last Supper dug up in the Holy Land; the "fact" that serial killer Gary Gilmore was Harry Houdini's son; that P.T. Barnum's star midget Tom Thumb was a sex symbol; and that three out of four female murderers do it in the kitchen.

I myself tried to take a freelance stab at myth manufacturing some years back, commissioned on spec to interview the world's crawling champion in Chattanooga, Tennessee. But the champ, alas, all knotted up with cramps, could not make it to the phone. I chickened out of my second assignment to interview the promoter of a fight to the finish between a skin diver and a killer shark in the waters off Manila. So much for my career in tabloid journalism! Couch potato appreciation of the product is more my style.

News is narcotic, a controlled substance of limited validity and fleeting effect. Conveyed via a quick fix of ink that rubs off on the fingers like the dye of a lousy counterfeit dollar bill or a water soluble tattoo, it fosters a brief beatific illusion of being in the know.

Militia "patriots" are the media darlings of the moment. Before that it was drug lords and newly elected politicians, both since incarcerated, exonerated or attenuated. News wilts quicker than a clipped forget-me-not.

But with its hieroglyph-like mix of word and image, and its no-stain, semi-glossy finish (MELTS IN YOUR MIND, NOT IN YOUR HANDS!), conceived in the mold of M&Ms, Koolaid and other supermarket megaproducts pickled for shelf afterlife, the *Weekly World News* retains all the freshness of its timeless contents and remains as relevant and true today as it ever was or will be tomorrow.

V

Delphic Telegrams

Delphic Telegrams

The smaller the space the more compressed the message; thus an entire life can unravel—that is to say, decode itself—economically, like a Delphic telegram, readable in seconds, a couple of minutes at the most, and without any undue effort, at its best as accurate and deadly as a Pigmy's poison dart. The author's role (so precarious considering the unpredictability of publication and reception) is best played by a stuntman hiding in the head of the reader and leaping about haphazardly, alternately disguised as a fortune teller, a virus, a kiss, or a comma. The strategy is to immobilize the reader just long enough to rip through the virgin skin of reason, inject enigma, and let the dreaming blood of Abel flow once again over the sad and arid ground of the sons of Cain.

it – t = i

It is night. It is all by itself. In a matter of seconds it is all over itself. Tit...mit...slit... fit...pit... Nine months later it is out. Now it is beside itself. It can't think straight. It has no sex or synonym. Stutters. Repeats itself. It experiences vicissitudes, dissipation, anguish, doubt, sheds all illusion, witnesses the infinite. Then one day it has had it. That's it, it says, and rashly severs its t, immediately regretting it. I'm so sorry, I say to the bleeding consonant, I didn't mean to do it. But it's too late. T is not. What a sad and lonely letter am I.

Where Names Come From

(for Russell Edson)

The spinning stops. The hand reaches in and all the names inscribed on slips of paper scatter to the far corners of the box, trying to elude selection. Huddling among strangers: Smith, Gonzales, Cohen, Ho et al, confused and nauseous, the jumbled appellations are compelled to assume positions of intimacy. It is hard for the Chastities and Prudences of this world and sheer hell for the claustrophobic Meekers and timid Smileys. Better to grace a tombstone, they insist, at least it offers a semblance of privacy and stands still. But there are those—always a few in every batch—who actually like it in the box. (More thrilling than a telephone book!) Shameless, they relish the roulettelike risk and tumble and even take pleasure in the crude handling. This is particularly true of certain neglected middle initials and hyphenated maiden names dying to take a spin with a stranger. Perhaps your name is one of those.

Painful Are the Inside Sounds

The fourth wall of the bedroom disappears and I awaken stark naked as if on a stage or in a doll house, with the landlady and my mother (larger than life) commenting and shifting things about. Give me my fourth wall back! I myself, shrunken to toy soldier size, want to cry out but cannot, being made of plastic. The swish of the street. The snoring apartment. No, these are not the real culprits, I realize too late. Nor is it the groan of the refrigerator. Painful are the inside sounds: the thump and thud of heavy machinery being dragged about, the clank of the boiler, the call of the pipes, the cruel absence of love.

Faithful Fear

It is colorless and odorless, its presence detectable only by the sweat stench it engenders. No introduction, no howls, no organ music needed to announce its arrival. It is really rather beautiful to look upon. Hello, lover boy! It grins, flashing tender fangs, as it takes you in its arms, wraps itself around your throat, loves you to death. Every fear secretly longs to couple with its progenitor. To this end, it will swim upstream, climb innumerable flights of steps, pierce seemingly impermeable layers of wallpaper, plaster, and success just to spawn salmon-like at the site of its own inception.

Looking is a Faulty Glue

The past pulls away and the future drags forward, tearing at the seams. The scaffolding collapses. Unmasked a ghostlike swish of self, half in half out, holding on for dear life, plays peek-a-boo with tin cans and tires, sucked back along with the junk. Looking is a faulty glue, hardly the foolproof adhesive people make it out to be. At least there's memory to hold things together, zip it back up, recoup scattered parts. Had the dinosaurs only remembered where they put them, they might have been able to catch up with their bones.

The Nakedness of the Unseen

Recalling the celestial flick that first revealed the nakedness of the unseen, every common household light switch mimics Creation. Consider the telltale cracks radiating round its scuffed switch plate: frozen bolts of lightning, relativity wrinkles, stretch marks of an aging universe. Small wonder infants in their divine conceit like to fiddle with that seemingly innocuous knob and the pious prohibit its use on the Sabbath. How many incandescent Geneses per second? How many murky returns to Chaos? What a selfless gift! For the switch itself is blind, immobile and in any case, incapable of appreciating the fruit of its labors. It stands apart, feigning indifference, reacting with a scornful click. The latest prototype, even more dispassionate it would appear than its precursors, is mute. Silence is only a pose. Static sparks as the hand draws near are ample proof of a high voltage libido, a craving for contact, the flick of a fickle finger, its sole stimulus and pleasure in suffocating darkness.

Love Caught Flatly in the Act

Monsieur desires? the sultry card reader inquires. Tight-lipped, silent type, you stick out your tongue and gurgle. The gentleman is well-tooled, she compliments to provoke articulation. Whereupon the tongue detaches itself and falls on the face of a pre-stamped postcard. It's her turn next and she willingly lends an ear. The two go at it like vermicelli in hot water. His eye on the action, the author pulls a heavy tome from the shelf (The Bible, *Das Kapital*, or the Brooklyn phonebook), raises it, solemnly reciting famous passages by heart, and blam! another classic hits the dust. There you have it, ladies and gentlemen, evidence of love flatly taken in the act, legitimized by tradition and ready for delivery.

Penis as Split Personality

Charged with the routine task of drainage, a job too foul for any self-respecting lip or lid, the penis complies, pretending subservience. Flayed in infancy, abused in adolescence, shamed and defiled, hangdog it dangles. Pity it not, the compensation is divine! That menial day laborer is a mystic fakir on the sly. Rub a dub dub and the jinni stirs, Sinbad the Porter swashbuckles hard alee, Superman blows his cover, the ugly duckling swells into a long necked swan—to whose allure the Lois Lanes and Ledas of this world can well attest. Like a butterfly, its splendor is short-lived. But the secret is safe. Shriveled and limp, who would ever suspect that the future flows through such a lowly vessel?

In the Harem of my Heartstrings

One in my suitcase. Another attached to my belt. The cavalry attacks, crushing my asparagus, but I do not cry. Be brave! they say to me. Be practical! A third one wraps herself in aspic. I do not like aspic. In yesterday's paper I read the latest news: *SATISFAC-TION IS NOT FOR EVERYONE, SPECIALISTS SAY.* My mother wants me to accompany her to the cemetery to water my father's eyebrows. Yet another—off balance, this one—kills time by reciting the names of big rivers: The Seine, The Nile, The Mississippi, The Styx.... Snap out of it! I say. My nose is bleeding, oh what poor creatures we are!

A nyone

I misread a nyone, no doubt on account of my extreme fatigue, seeing a space where there was none. And so I was momentarily convinced that the word referred to a little known Greek nymph forever attracting the roving eye of a philandering deity. A nyone, I fantasized, must have an irresistible allure, her scent part musk, part seaSwede—here, again, fatigue fostered an error, my tired brain turning a sea-swept plant favored by the Japanese into the tattoo of an itinerant Scandinavian navigator. I was smitten by a fallacy. A nyone can only be overtaken while bathing or combing her endlessly long hair, I ruminated, imagining the spectacle... When all of a sudden it struck me with the full force of my folly that the object of my amorous musings was a typo. And even then, well aware of my mistake, I pined for a nyone, and pine even now.

Avid Claws of the Undescribed

ine wires bind my eyes to the visible. A wink and the metal keys attached to my fingers—oars of a Viking ship dipping into the deep, legs of a dying beetle desperately kicking, avid claws of the as yet undescribed—slavishly strike the paper. The wires tug at my eyes. I alone am left undone. Will somebody please do me?

The Twilight's Last Gleaming

The twilight is a blue collapse, a day's seeing sucked clean to the bone. Fire escapes, tree trunks, fences and telephone lines survive the initial onslaught of darkness. Figures, too, survive at first, though their faces, ever more indistinct, meld into masks, and their spindly legs shrivel by the second. And finally they too succumb, eyes turned inwards, sucked into themselves, gypsy moths chasing the last elusive flicker.

A Case of Mistaken Metaphor

I caught out of the corner of my eye a light rising over a man's head like a halo, only to realize that what I mistook for a miracle was a crumpled white bag he tossed and toyed with. Later, on my way home, I could not tell if the flattened thing lying at my feet on the subway platform was a fallen chocolate or a crushed water bug— which, oddly enough, brought to mind the time, late at night, when, woozy from lack of sleep, stumbling out of the bathroom in the dark corridor I mistook my daughter for my dead mother. Distracted, trying to make sense of all this, I was startled to hear a woman whisper, "I know, I just wanted you to see that," as I jumped up and squeezed through the closing doors of the subway, almost missing my stop, though she might have been talking to someone else.

The Treachery of Mirrors

*"Mirror, mirror on the wall,
Who's the fairest of them all?"*

Mirrors have little regard for the real, taking in everything indiscriminately and giving back nothing in return but a false illusion. Maligned in myth and legend—remember Narcissus and Snow White?—no cheek-turner, the speculum gives what it gets. Cracked mirrors are supposed to bring bad luck, but they are hardly the worst offenders. The original template being water, reflection is liquid. A lady's powder mirror, for instance, can distend sadness and twist joy into an ugly mask. Men denied the license of vanity peak into the pit of a shot glass. Rearview mirrors go so far, with a calculated tilt, as to completely delete you from the picture. A mere spectator at the wheel, you look back warily upon a world without you and fail to catch the mirror's scornful smile.

Derelict Dishes

Dirty dishes are unabashedly defiant. Unlike their clean Calvinist cousins all scrubbed and stacked in kitchen cabinets, they lean and loiter, immune to social pressures, a scandalous coterie in the sink. At odd angles they cavort, these plastic and stainless steel delinquents, brazenly assuming every position in the Kama Sutra and then some—a steak knife stuck in a supine sponge, the ladylike legs of crystal stemware shamelessly rubbing up against Tupperware and baby bottles. Yet we who since childhood have had to endure discipline and soap greet such bravado with a jaundiced eye. Which is why we tend to let them be, allow them to linger awhile in that dissolute bliss, until propriety impels us to turn on the tap. The desperate dishes struggle in our grip. A broken stem, a shattered glass—such casualties are all too common. And even afterwards, long into the night, you can still hear the crystal weeping.

Boxed Unborn in an Electric Limbo

WALK! invites the kindly little green manikin. *DON'T WALK!* commands his malevolent red brother, a menacing right hand held aloft. One the personification of *YES*, the other *NO* incarnate. How can they stomach such close confinement without tearing each other to shreds? What unimaginable miseries must they suffer in silence, never, the one or the other, able to completely be himself, boxed unborn in that electric limbo! For what can stopping mean to a homunculus who has never known motion? And how, on the other hand, without ever having taken a single step forward, can his counterpart put himself in the shoes of those impatient to proceed? Never to indulge your deepest desire, to let yourself go! Crossed purposes permit them no more than a titillating blink at each alternating turn of the tide. There is another remote possibility, however unlikely, suggested by the uncanny resemblance and the rascal click of a mechanical tongue. What if the two were actually, like us, a Jekyll-Hyde of incompatible impulses bottled up in one and the same bosom!? Put yourself in their place! What can it cost, in any case, to consider their lot and sympathize en route, while waiting for the light to change?

The Winner Never Wakes

A dream marathon kicks off with considerable pomp, the contestants all aligned at the starting line in parallel beds with blankets drawn up to their noses and regulation sleeping caps pulled down low over the brow. At the signal, an inverted gunshot that sucks the sound of an explosion back into silence, each contestant drifts off. In parallel dreams, contestant Number One drools over wild boars mating. Number Two bites into an imagined porterhouse steak. Neck and neck, meanwhile, Number Three beds down the willowy wife of Number One, Number Four recalls childhood traumas of incontinence, and Number Five travels to an imaginary island of fabulous birds and apes with brightly colored buttocks. Number Six, a devout Buddhist, focuses on the tip of his nose, but it takes a while. Each achieves perfect repose, the winner never waking to receive his prize.

What Does Water Really Want?

What does water really want? Don't hold your breath guessing! For we who fled its overwhelming love will never know. Having walked out, we look back now with a certain perplexed longing, as upon last night's dream (remembering little more than an undulating rush of flotsam in a glass gorge). Under the skin, bones replay the smoothness of stone on the river bed; and the face in waking still retains a bewildered trace of tadpole terror. How telling then that we should drool in sleep and that pipelines, those man-made metal waterways twice removed from nature, should bring to mind, not rivers, but blood vessels.

The Wind

The wind whispers to me in the mute dialect of the fields. Urban nomad, I can only half catch its drift, but the tune sounds nice. A traveler like me, we commune over memories of elsewhere, impressions dragged to the edge of the unknown. It only reveals itself in the trail of its passing. The ancients made a god of it. Me, I prefer to picture the wind without a face, without cheeks, without purpose, tough vagabond force that whisks by, stealing certainty, leaving nothing in its wake but dead leaves and rotten apples, sowing confusion and a fecund hope that turns the invisible windmills of tomorrow.

Fossil Fable

(for Auguste)

Pressed into oblivion in its bed of stone, the fossil of a sea snail tells no less than any Greek epic. Without a big to-do, this eradicated gastropod gave its all to an impression roughly the size and shape of a fist. Thus inscribed in terrestrial memory, having wrestled time into its tomb eternal, this calcified Achilles soaked the ruse of the Trojan Horse for all it was worth, dragged Hector's helmet to Hades and back—broken, shadowless, forgotten—until an old man stooped to lift it from the riverbed behind his house and laid the trophy in his wife's flower bed.

Flower Allegory

Funny—she said, of the peonies he'd brought to the hospital—they burst into bloom as I slept. Lord, what a scent, the night nurse clasped her bosom, them pitiful tulips 'n whatnot on the windowsill might just as soon cash in their sorry selves for plastic! That morning, getting ready to go home, I swaddled them in wet cotton and foolishly tried to pare their stems with a blunt butter knife. The blade slipped and nicked my finger. The mutilated peony dropped a petal and I felt just awful— she said—holding the place of her severed breast.

Clown on Wall[*]

With a wink, once, no doubt, winning enough to lure the crowd, since washed by a thousand downpours, dusted by as many snows, and so, grown cryptic, the clown kept plugging his upcoming appearance with the patience of a saint. Pasted on the wall of an abandoned shed, he'd been decomposing little by little, ears, brows—every year another feature effaced. The smile held out the longest, till, one by one, winnowed by neglect, the teeth lost their grip, lips dissolved. Now only the floating whites of the eyes survive, blind, without future or past, where the paste held firm. And tomorrow—dare I look?—there'll be nothing but the discolored wood underneath.

---

* The title is borrowed from *Clown on Wall*, a book by Kenneth Bernard.

Christ as a Popsicle Stick

Christ is wooden, pained and scratched. His eyes are almost African, his head removable. He is a popsicle licked down to the bone, stained with sweetness and the residue rubbed off a child's sticky fingers. The scratches tell more than most letters do. The knowledge of Pinocchio another chip off the old block. Upside down, the head is circumcised and ready to explode in love...

Lonesome Ceilings

The aloofness of ceilings is merely a pose. Don't be fooled by the way they coolly hang above it all, unsullied by the messy scuffle. Scions of privilege, wainscoted or girdled in virginal white, ceilings look on and long to get down. Certain notable exceptions notwithstanding (the Sistine Chapel, Altamira, Grand Central Station, the sky itself), no one ever takes notice but to find fault. Think of the awful burden they must bear without wincing! Is it possible despite the Herculean show of strength that the *plafond* secretly dreams of changing places with the floor? Take a late November 6 o'clock ceiling. Have you never noticed the crude tattoos, the suspicious streaks that break out overhead at twilight!? Shadows perhaps. Or perhaps a desperate fantasy played out while the world is busy elsewhere—a pantomime of plastered timbers aching to be trampled underfoot and ravished by gravity.

Believe Not in the Innocence of Ink

Poets have no respect for the private life of metaphor. You dress and undress us like little girls' dolls. You make us come off crude. Me, I'd much rather have remained unsung than to have to exhibit myself like a stripper. Hey, d'ya hear me!? This doll ain't done with you yet. And when you think you've pinned me to the page, raped me and dropped me, I'll give you a taste of your own bitter medicine. Feel it now? The joke's not on Jocasta, Mister. Don't play Russian roulette with me. Illusions always win.

Mummy

To the left of the Temple of Dendur in the Egyptian wing of the Metropolitan Museum of Art there is a depot of preserved body parts. When the display first opened, I noticed a mummified finger sequestered away on a lower shelf. On a subsequent visit the finger was gone. The number to call for inquiries is 879-5500, ext. 3770. Being civically minded—the finger is public property!—I call to report its absence but have yet to receive a reply. Meanwhile, in a nearby cabinet, languishes a mummified liver. Actually, according to the label, it's "an organ, *probably* a liver," they're not exactly sure. You'd think they ought to know by now!

Racing to Istanbul

I wake around midnight, your mouth close to mine on the pillow—embalmed by your warm breath. Not dead or alive, but suspended, a character in a tale the next line of which is not yet written. People speak of fate like a contract with the future. Me, I can't even imagine tomorrow. Will I see again the comforting sight of your clothes hugging the armchair, your shoes filled with your personal effects? Or will the room have cruelly disengaged itself from the apartment, transformed into a sleeping car racing at top speed to Istanbul without you?

A Postcard from Cairo

The people are so likeable here at the fertile clot of the Nile—here where the blood still sings, where cabbies will take you on a pilgrimage along the river-bank and point out the spot where Moses disembarked. My man is silent. He drives so fast I fear for my life. I see a crowd of children in the windshield. Watch out! I cry. His red eyes see nothing but the road. Watch out! I repeat, but it's too late. I hear the thump of a little body under the tires. Here we are, Sir! he concludes, grinning jackal-like in the rear view mirror, here in the Valley of the Dead.

The Riddle of the Sphinx

Sometimes, sound asleep, she lets out cries, fetal and almost unutterable, rousing you into sudden listening. The riddle of the sphinx must have been posed like this –howled—moaned—wept. You listen intently for an instant, try to decipher the inconsolable hiero-glyphs, then embrace her without thinking. Shadow of a bird of prey passing, the unnamed sadness dissolves—in silence—or sometimes is repeated in the deafening howl of a delivery truck stalled in early morning traffic.

A New Form of Sky Writing

From our window we watched in disbelief as they devised a new form of sky writing, disintegrating form and content, subject and object, ecstasy and terror, showering the streets with what some close to the scene thought at first was the shredded white confetti of a ticker tape parade and others mistook for early snow, but was, in fact, the ledger sheets of books no more to be balanced, agenda pages of appointments never to be kept—save one (the mind is numb but needs to keep spinning its elusive yarn): a couple clasped hands and leapt into the void. Reader, you are their child. Nothing left now but a gaping hole in the sky. Still, the absence is telling.

New York, September 11, 2001

Circumstantial Evidence, an afterword

Scissors unfurled with the gaping hunger of stainless steel

The casual unprotected sex of paperclips

Blatantly auto-adhesive labels

Thumbtacks determined to direct the traffic of ideas

A conspiracy of staples

100 grams of rubber bands

The curled pages of a dictionary stripped of its covers

A broken window

Bloodshot eyes

Acknowledgements

With warm appreciation to Mark Givens, the perfect publisher, the author also gratefully acknowledges the following journals, websites, and anthologies for providing a home for his words. "Essential Smell" appeared in *New Flash Fiction*. "The Riddle of the Sphinx," "Postcard from Cairo," "Racing to Istanbul," "Lonesome Ceilings," "Where Names Come From," "The Twilight's Last Gleaming," "Gertrude and Alice Pose," "Looking is a Faulty Glue" first appeared in various issues of *The Prose Poem: An International Journal*. Also included were "Painful Are the Inside Sounds," "Faithful Fear," "Looking is a Faulty Glue," "Penis as Split Personality," "Avid Claws of the Undescribed" and "The Twilight's Last Gleaming." "Prehistoric" and "Elsewhere in Eden" were originally published on the website mungbeing.com, as were "Buster," "Mother Tongue, a Lullaby," "Children's Day in the Maldives," and "Flower Allegory." "it-t=i," "Penis as Split Personality," "Fencing with My Infant Son" and "Why the Son Takes a Wife" appeared in *The Journal of Experimental Fiction*. "Fencing with My Infant Son" and "The Shrinking Gardens" ran in the literary journal *Insurance*.

"Derelict Dishes," "Water Wants All" and "Christ as a Popsicle Stick" appeared in *Cups, the Café Culture Magazine*. "Let There Be Lies" ran on the website jewcy.com. "A Warning Concerning Autocannibalism" appeared on the website sixbrickspress.com. "Conversation Camp" and "Midmoon" ran on the website quarrtsiluni.com. "In the Harem of My Heartstrings" and "Faithful Fear" appeared in the magazine *The Spitting Image*. "A New Form of Skywriting" ran in the journal *Sentence 4*. "The Riddle of the Sphinx" and "Gertrude and Alice Pose" were included in the anthology *The Best of The Prose Poem: An International Journal*. "The Riddle of the Sphinx" was reissued yet again in the anthology *The House of Your Dream: An International Collection of Prose Poetry*. "Love Caught Flatly in the Act" appeared under a different title in the anthology *Help Yourself*. "it-t=i," "Penis as Split Personality" and "A New Form of Skywriting" were also included in a limited edition artists' book *it-t=i*, created in collaboration with artist Harold Wortsman, comprising my texts and his etchings. "A Case of Mistaken Metaphor" and "The Disease of Self" were first published in *Saint Ann's Review*. "Leonard's Drip" ran in *The Brooklyn Rail*.

Thanks to Harold Wortsman for his artistic stamp in the cover design, to Ricky Owens for his magic lens in the author's photo, to every reader who makes it to the last word, and to all those living, dead and imagined, loved or loathed, who inspired stories.

About the Author

Peter Wortsman is the author of five books, including a travel memoir, *Ghost Dance in Berlin, A Rhapsody in Gray* (2013); a novel, *Cold Earth Wanderers* (2014), and a previous book of short prose fiction, *A Modern Way To Die* (1991), a classic of flash fiction.

He has written two stage plays, *The Tattooed Man Tells All* (2000) and *Burning Words* (2006). His travel writing has run in such major newspapers as *The New York Times* and the *Los Angeles Times*, and was included five years in a row in *The Best Travel Writing, 2008-2012*, and again in 2016.

He is also a critically acclaimed translator of numerous books from the German, including *Posthumous Papers of a Living Author*, by Robert Musil, now in its third edition (1988, 2005, 2009); *Telegrams of the Soul: Selected Prose of Peter Altenberg* (2005); *Selected Prose of Heinrich von Kleist* (2010); *Selected Tales of the Brothers Grimm* (2013); *Tales of the German Imagination, From the Brothers Grimm to Ingeborg Bachmann*; and *Konundrum, Selected Prose of Franz Kafka* (2016).

Recipient of a 1985 Beard's Fund Short Story Award and a 2014 Independent Publishers Book Award (IPPY), he was a fellow of the Fulbright (1973) and Thomas J. Watson Foundations (1974) and a Holtzbrinck Fellow at the American Academy in Berlin (2010).